STIRRED *Up*

Nikki—
my love
for you is
more than words!

Angela

STIRRED

S.E. Hall

&

Angela Graham

Table of Contents

Coming together is a beginning; keeping together is progress; working together is success.

—Anonymous

Chapter One

"DYLAN!" I bang louder now, rolling my eyes, half-tempted to add in a few kicks as well.

Every attempt I make to visit, he takes his sweet ass time opening the damn door. I usually don't let it rattle me but it was free spay and neuter day at the vet clinic where I work and I'm exhausted. All I want to do is peel these pinching shoes off my aching feet and sit down with a cold beer and a slice of pizza while catching up with my big brother.

If he'd turn down his incessant video game and come answer the door, that is.

My fist hammers against the wood again and still nothing. Heaving out an exasperated huff, I sling my work bag around my shoulder, balancing our steaming dinner and tall boys in my hands as I dig inside my purse for the spare key he gave me on move in day a year earlier.

"Dylan!" Yelling again, I try to peer through the window. If he's got that headphone thing on that he uses to talk to other gamers, I could be here all night. With no luck on the hunt for his elusive key, I pull out my phone instead. *He's so buying next time.*

"Addison, dear."

I whirl around, startled, nearly dropping my phone and everything else I'm holding at the sound of the voice. It's sweet Mrs. Murray from the apartment across the way.

"Your brother's gone," she continues. "He and that handsome friend of his were moving things out all day."

Brady. Rescuing my meandering brother again.

I shove my phone back in my purse, struggling to tame my aggravated scowl long enough to give the elderly, helpful woman a smile. "Thank you, Mrs. Murray, and sorry for the noise."

The familiar ache builds in my temples, the one only

two guys ever cause, consistently stressing me out with some shenanigan or another.

"Not at all, honey. If I don't see you kids again, you all take care."

My shoulders slump when she closes the door. Unable to contain my frustration, I stomp the entire way out of the building and straight to my car, where I toss the dinner and drinks onto the passenger seat a little too hard. Once I'm buckled up and ready to go, I inhale a deep breath and take my anger out on the steering wheel.

What the hell is wrong with him? With both of them?

I'm livid, and pretty sure most of my fellow drivers take notice as I weave in and out of traffic way too fast, risking my perfect driving record. I don't care and I don't stop, besides at the one red light that I swear is mocking me, all the way to Brady's house, ready to lay into them both. Far too annoyed to be bothered with knocking, I crash through the front door and slam the now-cold pizza and warm beer on the table in the entryway.

"Jackasses, I'm home!" I yell out into the large house, balancing on first one, then the other leg to finally take off my shoes. Heaven forbid I traipse further into the way-too-big-for-one-single-man's house with my shoes on. Brady's by far the more hygienic one of the duo, my brother more of a quick rinse, anything on the floor not stiff enough to stand on its own is still wearable kind of guy. It's the main reason they've never made good roommates and the first point I'll be making if they think they can hole up together again.

"In the living room," Dylan calls back, obviously too busy to walk the ten steps to greet me.

Irritation climbs straight to homicidal rage in seconds when I turn the corner and see them. Seemingly unconcerned with his recent unannounced move, my brother is sprawled out in a beanbag, fingers tapping rapid-fire on his controller…not a care in the world. Brady, the enabler, is relaxed in the armchair with a white blanket spread over his lap, his head dipped back, eyes closed, a wicked curl to his lips. The girly feet peeking out from under the blanket tell me I'm definitely interrupting, not that I care, but I'm appalled that Dylan is so far lost in his game that he hasn't noticed the blowjob happening a few feet to his left.

Brady releases a low grunt, his hips shooting up, hands

gripping the blanket, which is actually the head of Casper the Friendly Cocksucker, as she finishes him off. The thought of what just slid down her throat causes some bile to rise in mine; *seriously, there's a guy sitting right beside you and your escapade soundtrack is squawking video game birds—talk about hot.*

I give the back of his chair a swift kick and move across the room, not wanting a close-up of that show. "Sorry to bust up the frat party," I chirp sarcastically, "but does anybody want to tell me why Dylan's homeless *again?*"

"Hey, Moe." Brady's hands disappear under the fabric, pushing whoever's done there away and raising his hips to tuck what I can only assume is his dick back in a more appropriate place. Instantly, a busty girl crawls out from between his legs, wiping her thumb across her swollen lips. She stands, pushing the blanket to the floor, and I catch a glimpse of Brady zipping up his fly. He's all smiles when he looks over at me. "Do I smell sausage or pepperoni?"

His *guest* attempts to sit on his lap, but is brutally rebuffed as he's already sauntering toward me with that signature cocky gait of his.

Widening my stance defensively, I cross my arms over

my rapidly rising and falling chest and narrow my eyes at him. "Why did Dylan move out of his apartment, and *why the hell* is he staying here?"

He walks right past me, leaving me waiting, which I hate, until he reappears a moment later, beer and pizza in hand.

"You're cute when you're pissy, Moe." He winks at me and taps the end of my nose.

I make to knock his finger away but it's already gone. God knows where it's been today. I grimace at the fleeting thought.

"Thanks for dinner, but the beer…you know I don't drink this girly shit. Although tonight…." He dangles the six pack of Bud Light Lime from his fingers like it's toxic.

I try to grab it but he isn't letting go. I'm well aware they don't drink it, precisely why I brought it. I like to actually enjoy a drink or two, not watch them chug it all down, so I'm shocked when he cracks one open.

"What the—"

"All day in the operating room. Gimme a break. But if you say please, I'll pour one for you myself," Brady says smugly.

"Let go and I won't spit on your slice," I quip back. No way am I saying please.

He thinks it over, still holding the beer in one hand, pointer finger tapping his chin with the other. "Hmm, something tells me I've tasted your spit before and yet I still live so—"

"Not like you never deserved it, Mr. Come On In, the Water's Only Waist Deep!"

His lips curl up into a reminiscent smirk, eyes bright as he releases his death grip on my refreshments. "Poor Dylan almost drowned, holding me up while you debated forever. Fuck, was that funny, though. Three steps and *whoosh*, you were totally under."

"Bring me a slice already," Dylan yells, never breaking his trance on the screen.

"Get your own!" Brady and I yell back in sync.

I roll my eyes, laughing softly with Brady. The ease of our amusement is cut short, though.

"Oh, that's my favorite!" the pouty lipped bimbo squeals, strolling over with a broad, eager beam, eyeing my beer. *Hell no!* "Hi, I'm Candace. You must be Moe."

My scowl is back. "My *name* is Addison," I grit out.

"Only since your hair grew out, *Moe*," Brady tugs on one of my curls playfully.

"I don't get it?" Bimbo says, looking even more confused, if that's possible.

"*The Three Stooges?* Moe used to rock a bowl cut when she was little." He grips his side, laughing.

She still doesn't get it and never will, given her blank stare, and the whole conversation's grating on my nerves. "Let me guess, you go by Candy?" I ask her.

"I do, yeah." She affirms proudly.

Shocker. I have no words nice enough to respond with so instead I step around her, plopping down on the couch, tossing one of the pillows at Dylan's head.

What grown man hangs out in beanbags, in the early evening of a workday, while his best friend, also grown, mangles a co-ed? Am I the only one (the youngest to boot) in our little trio who ever grew up?

"Here," I look up to find Brady holding out the frozen mug he keeps in the freezer for me, "don't make me eat alone."

I glance at the girl in his kitchen opening and closing cabinets, wondering what the hell she's looking for and when she's leaving.

"Where's your plates?" she finally calls out.

"You're far from alone but feel free to bring me a slice." I grin, then turn my attention back to my brother's game.

Brady's hot breath hits the back of my ear. "I knew you'd be coming so I picked up your favorite."

I tilt my head his direction, finding him bent down, his face inches from mine. I can't deny that the man drew the pretty stick. With enough alcohol in me, you might even coerce a confession that I once had a semi-crush on him. Thing is, when I say once, I mean over fifteen years ago when I was about eleven. That all disappeared when he decided to join my brother as the dynamic duo of tormentors who created their very own version of *Fear Factor*...where I was the only contestant every damn episode. Since then, he'd become the bane of my existence.

"Strawberry Jell-O," he murmurs, his lips twitching upward.

Damnit, I do love Jell-O and he's the only one that makes it exactly how I like, adding a thin layer of banana slices on top. Despite his massive kitchen, it's the only thing he *can* make and I've never been able to resist.

Huffing loudly, I accept, allowing him to pull me to my feet and into the kitchen. "He get fired?" I ask lowly, as though my brother's even listening over his enthralling game in there.

"It's not what you think." He grabs the biggest, cheesiest slice, shooting me the knowing grin that I took inventory and noticed. "Have a little faith in him, would ya? His manager's been gunning for him since he figured out Dylan's better than-"

"I believe in him!" I shriek, interrupting and not caring. How could he suggest I don't? "But I also believe in getting the next door open *before* closing the last one," I continue. "He's always rebuilding, never moving up. And you," I glare and poke his chest, "make it too easy for him. He's thirty years old, for Christ's sake! Quit coddling him!"

His features soften, as does the smile he throws me. "I'm just helping him get back on his feet. He can do great things, Moe, all he needs is someone to believe in him and the right opportunity to come along."

Not a smart girl, Jezebel slides into my peripheral, plate in hand, and sneaks a piece of pizza. My eyes narrowing predatorily, I pin her in place.

"One piece, got it? I don't have to buy ya dinner, Sweet pea," I seethe, meeting her shocked, widened eyes. "*I didn't fuck ya.*"

"Neither did I!" Dylan yells from the living room. "I'll take her piece if you throw her out!"

Unbelievable. We discuss his life, he hears nothing. Bitch tries to short him food, he's all ears.

"Cookie," Brady coos at her sickeningly. That's what he calls them all—Cookie—since we were teenagers, because he can't remember their names. "You better be going."

She drops the slice back in the box and I return to my own cheesy goodness, satisfied and fully aware I've become a bitch. These two guys bring it out of me, so I place full blame on them and maybe a little on the fact that it's been over twelve months since I've had a man's hands anywhere near my body. I close my eyes, needing to unwind; unfortunately the yapping girl won't allow that.

"But, we didn't finish studying," she pouts, hands on hips, obviously fake chest poofed out in offering to him.

I swallow a bite and peer over at Brady, who's sitting

across from me now, refusing to acknowledge her whining. "Another nurse?" I sneer, one eyebrow judgmentally raised.

"Civic duty." He shrugs with a devilish grin, biting off a grotesquely big mouthful of pepperoni heaven.

"Hmph," I scoff, "as if you teach them anything medicinal."

"Oh, but he did," Blondie bounces, ticking the "lessons" off of her fingers. "He taught me the five points of restraint, how to take vitals and," she ponders, "oh yeah, breasts exams!"

My head snaps to Brady, eyes narrowed. "Restraints and breast exams, really?"

"Covering the basics." He winks.

I turn back to Blondie. "Candy, did he show you anything that's actually *on* your test, or did he just want to grope your tits?"

"No, no, no, breast exams are super important. He taught me a lot, want me to show you? I could use the practice!"

Is this *child* for real? I may only be twenty-six years old, but I was smarter than her at, say…five.

My penetrating glare moves from Brady to her. "If your hand comes anywhere near my girls, Goldilocks, you'll be pulling back a nub."

Brady snorts, choking through his laughter, and Nurse Whore is immediately at the ready to clap him on the back.

"Like, really though," she looks at me, pleadingly, "they're super important. You need to do them. Right Brady?"

"I appreciate your concern, but I have a doctor for that," I deadpan.

She bounces again. "Who?"

"Yeah, Moe, who?" Brady asks, recovered and lethally serious.

Shit, how did we get on this subject exactly? "Um, just a doctor." I glance away instinctively. "It's none of your business anyway," I add on a mumble, grabbing another slice and stomping off to the couch.

This day quickly went from hectic to bad to downright nightmarish. Brady reads me like the back of his hand, he's had sixteen years of experience, so I know that he knows I'm full of shit…a lecture is definitely on its way. Bracing for it, I stuff my face, dipping my head to conceal my staring as I watch Brady help Ditzy gather her things and lead her out.

The minute I've relaxed a bit, Brady drops beside me. Ugh, way too close, so I can smell *her* over his classic scent of confidence and man. "You still mad at me?" he leans in and whispers in my ear, earning him a swift elbow to the ribs.

"Is she old enough to drive herself home?"

His head falls back, exposing his taut, tan throat with his laugh. "Yep. Smart enough to have regular exams too. I know you, Moe, your try at evasive doesn't work on me." His voice levels to a chastising, low timbre, his green eyes boldly holding mine. "It pisses me off to think you don't take care of yourself. Women's bodies are complex, fascinating things; there's lots to take care of."

"Why is it such a big deal? I'm only twenty-six years old and it's not like I'm working the streets at night."

"It's a big deal." His stern voice leaves no room for argument.

"Sir, yes, sir, I'll get right on that," I salute, shutting down the conversation. I go grab Dylan another slice, his hand already out when I arrive at the beanbag throne.

"You bet your ass you will," Brady calls out and I try to ignore exactly what that means. He's the most persistent man alive, scarily stubborn and renowned for getting his way…especially when it comes to his friends' health.

Chapter Two

"WELL HELLO THERE, Mimi," I coo at the brilliant scarlet macaw when I walk in the next morning. The clinic "pet," she's allowed to roam free overnight. "Who's a pretty bird?"

"Mimi's a pretty bird," she responds, flying over to perch on my shoulder.

I flip on the lights and set down my bags, turning the blinds to open as my cell phone begins trilling from my purse.

"Tell her I'm not here, tell her I'm not here," Mimi sing-songs.

I roll my eyes, snickering. Dr. Burns, the town vet I work for, married almost sixty years now, taught the bird that phrase as a passive-aggressive dig at his beloved wife. He thinks it's hilarious.

"Hello?" I answer, slowly, unsure of the caller.

"Ms. Porter?"

My brows pinch. "This is Addison Porter."

"Good morning, this is Whitney from Dr. Reynolds' office. I'm calling to confirm your appointment for tomorrow morning at 10 am."

Appointment? It hits me in two flat seconds. *Brady.* Shaking my head, I blow out a breath. I should have known that condescending bastard wouldn't let up, but making an appointment for me?! Why am I even surprised? And because this tiny, off the grid town has only one gynecologist, *of course* it's at Dr. Reynolds' office! Never been and never planned to go, but suddenly faced with it, I need to take a minute to consider my options.

There are only two choices—drive thirty-five minutes to the next town, the closest thriving metropolis, defined as such because it boasts both a Taco Bell *and* a Wal-Mart, and bring Brady back a "proof of pap" note, or…

"I'll be there," I manage brightly into the receiver.

"Wonderful, see you then."

I disconnect that call, and am feverishly dialing the next one when my coworker, Maggie, breezes through the door. I guess Brady's reaming will have to wait.

"ARE YOU KIDDING ME, Brady? Presumptuous much? Who makes other people's doctor appointments for them?" I growl into the phone the moment I step outside the office for my lunch.

Know it all, wannabe big brothers who are doctors themselves—that's who.

His tone is stern, making himself clear as he lays it out. "I wasn't kidding, Moe, you can't play around with that stuff. And don't even think about cancelling."

Yeah right, like I'd let him see me sweat! I may have been the wind to his and Dylan's wings growing up, always the shy, bookish little sister tagging along in their shadows, but I'm a grown woman now! I may very well strut into that appointment naked, wrapped in twinkle lights! My life, my vagina…I say who, I say when!

That'll show 'em!

"Oh, I won't," I challenge. "Bet on it."

"Good." Triumph annoyingly evident in his voice. "So what's that blonde coworker of yours with the tight ass wearing today?"

"Nothing she'll let you near again!" I hang up in his ear, smiling gleefully to myself that I got the last word.

The victorious grin I boast is short-lived. As usual.

Only seconds later, my text dings and without even looking I know, *I just know*, who it is. Argh, that man!! See, now even if I don't look, *he* doesn't know I didn't look, and he's still won!

Brady: Last word infinity.

A bubble of laughter catches in my throat as I shake off the grin I can't help. And I wonder why he's the first person Dylan runs to when being a grown up proves too much? They were made for each other; brothers by blood don't have a thing on them.

Releasing some of the anxiety fluttering through me over the appointment, my shoulders drop and my head falls back to rest on the brick wall of the building. What did I get myself into? Any time Brady has control over something in my life, I get burned. I close my eyes, sighing as my mind replays the last disaster courtesy of my so-called buddy.

It was a pottery class, a birthday gift from him that he even agreed to attend with me. Less than twenty minutes in, he was bashing the hot young male instructor for his overly friendly help to the female students, me being one of them. Not that I minded, did I mention he was hot?

Brady pinned the guy with his pointed glare each time he came near me to offer assistance and cracked constant jokes about the guy being a putz a little too loudly. The case cracker, however, was Brady's "the man needs to bend her over already" comment that got him physically removed from class. Turns out the "her" in question and Teacher were actually a couple, happily married. And me— sitting pretty, hands gooey, loving the vase I was slowly creating—was shown the door before I could finish. Why? Because of Mr. I Know Everything and Can't Keep my Opinions to My Damn Self.

Despite the past, Brady's a huge part of my life and I'd give in this one time, but not without leveling the playing field a little. With only ten minutes left in the lunch break that Brady managed to hijack, a sinister, but brilliant, idea hits me and I act before I can talk myself out of it.

"Hello?"

"Kathy? Hi, it's Addison Porter, how are you?" I grip the phone tightly, excitement coursing through me.

Thanks to the Brady flu disaster of '03, I conveniently have his housekeeper's number... too tempting to resist. I'd spent an entire weekend pampering him, sick in bed, only to collapse down beside him in the end. Luckily, he was coming out of his sweat-induced fog just as I was heading into it. The familiar shiver races up from my spine, recalling how he held me in his arms, kissed my forehead, and promised to take care of me. And he did, showering me with unwavering tenderness for the rest of the week. He held my hair while I emptied my stomach, continuously cooled the washcloth he pressed to my fevered skin, and fed me my favorite soup. Despite his herculean efforts, we still needed Kathy for drug store runs, bless her heart.

"Well, I'm fine, dear. How are you?" She's such a nice woman; I come *this close* to nixing the whole plan and making up a random excuse for the call.

This close.

"I'm good, thank you. I was calling for Brady, he's tied

up in cases today. Dylan's staying with him for a while and really wants to earn his keep, so Brady thought it'd be nice to give you all next week off and let Dylan take care of it."

"A week off?" She breathes out wistfully, evidently already imagining ways to spend the free time. "I could go visit my son."

"You should!" *Easy there, Addison, not too obvious.* "I'm sure he'd love to see you."

"Yes, that's what I'll do. This is wonderful, please tell Brady and Dylan both thank you."

"Of course I will. You have fun, don't worry about us, or about calling Brady. I'll tell him we spoke and how excited you are. In fact, don't even take your phone with you, Kathy, escape for a while and enjoy your family."

"You know, I think I will. Thank you, dear," she says brightly, her excitement ringing through.

The day my brother keeps his own shit picked up, let alone cleans an entire house, and for a week, I'll give up chocolate and chick flicks. Those two Neanderthals are gonna be swimming in filth by tomorrow night, mark my words. The mere thought makes me giddy, erasing my earlier aggravation and making the rest of the day bearable.

Infinity sminity—take that, Mr. Appointment Maker.

———⚓———

NEVER ONCE have I felt as out of sorts as I do standing in front of the feminine hygiene products. Gone is the whistling, carefree girl that strolled in the store, still basking in the torture she'd sprung on an unsuspecting friend. Here I am in the corner drug store where I came for fresh razors but the damn "Feminine" sign drew me over. My eyes and brain can hardly keep up; there are *way* too many products available for the vagina.

"Excuse me," a woman says out of nowhere, reaching for the douche kit in front of me.

I smile and take one myself, tossing it into my cart. *Totally normal.* I can do this. Unsure what the other items are, I pluck one from each category and hightail it to the front of the store. Waiting in line, I snatch a bottle of lotion from the display. Jasmine works for me; in the cart it goes.

What I had not anticipated when I'd filled my cart with half a dozen freshening products was the young cashier, of course male, currently straining to control his amusement as he scans each item slowly. *Yeah, yeah, I like a clean vagina; keep scanning, buddy.* I thrust the cart forward and begin bagging the items myself.

Chapter Three

I WAKE with a lead weight in my gut, the panic of today's looming appointment sinking in the minute my eyes peel open. Nope, not ready to face it. I slam my eyes shut again, roll to my stomach, and bury my face in my pillow. My nerves are alive and rampant, eating at me to hurry up before the clock runs out and I'm left going to the appointment unshaved with the stench of the vet's office lingering.

With a huff, I'm on my feet shuffling to the bathroom. This is it—V day. No, not the flowers and candy one, the vagina one. I glance back at my cell phone perched mockingly on my night stand, my only escape plan. Beads of cold sweat break out over my forehead and the base of my neck, hell, even my breasts are damp. They're not ready to play peek-a-boo with the doc, let alone be fondled and judged. The debate to call and cancel is off the table. I already took the morning off work and my health *is* important, not to mention I'll walk across fire and snakes—*snakes on fire*—before I let Brady win!

Cursing him under my breath, I grab the two full bags of products and slam the bathroom door behind me. If I'm gonna do this, I'm gonna do it right. I turn on the shower to let it warm up and start with the easiest task, brushing my teeth. A little floss, mouthwash, spit and voila! Pearly whites glisten back in the mirror.

After opening the new pack of razors, I strip out of my clothing and dig under the counter for the hand mirror. Because of the *ample* notice I'd gotten, obviously there's no time for a professional visit, so ladyscaping is left up to me. I'm not that worried, the work should be light considering I keep a monthly appointment at our local spa, but with my love life nonexistent as such, I need to fully assess the situation.

Focused more on my lackluster dating life, I grab the few feminine products that I can apparently use in the tub. I step one foot into the shower and instantly rear back with a trembling squeal when the scalding stream hits my toes.

"Crap!" I reach in to crank the nozzle a bit, cursing my lousy apartment building for the always unpredictable water heater.

Timidly, I poke a finger into the downstream and relax for the first time all morning. Gotta take the small victories. Easing into the warm shower, I first tend to the basics, hair washing, loofah scrubbing, and armpit shaving. Next my legs, twice, with my usual silky body butter, using long, smooth strokes, willing my hands to stop shaking; the last thing I need is a ton of little nicks from my pesky nerves.

With an expert eye, not a single sneaky loner hair around my ankle or hidden behind my knee is left untouched. And then, in the most limberly-challenged way possible, I prop my right leg up with my foot on the edge of the tub, mirror gripped in one hand, razor in the other.

This is it, one stray hair left in the wrong place or a tiny nick will reveal my anxious preparation. Not the time for haste. I duck my head so water doesn't hit my eyes and give my girl a slight trim, nothing over the top. She looks pretty good actually, so the job's fairly easy, but with the obstacles and my anxiety, it takes longer than it should.

When I'm completely satisfied she's show worthy, I release a cleansing breath and turn off the spray, which was growing colder by the minute. I wrap myself in the comfort of my favorite extra-large fluffy towel, surprisingly, another birthday gift from Brady. He got tired of me complaining that the perfect towel didn't exist. Turns out I was wrong, Brady found it, and bought me a whole stack, which had me in awe, especially when I went to the store he'd purchased them in and saw the price tag.

Perfect or not, it was out of my budget.

Clean, check. Smooth, check. What next? Deodorant! I go ahead and slather it on now so it'll have time to dry, then sit on the lid of my toilet and open the first shopping bag.

Like a grab bag, I reach in blindly and pull out a deodorant, but not for my underarms. I flip it over and read the back. "Island splash. Spray anytime you need that fresh feeling."

Sounds easy enough. Ripping the package open, I give

a little test squirt in the air and I'm hit with the scent of coconuts. Not too offensive, subtle and clean. Unsure of the appropriate distance to hold it, I spread my legs and spray. The coolness covers my sex, tingling the sensitive flesh. Definitely feeling fresh. Thumbs up there.

I place it on the counter and pull out the second product, wipes. Not needed, I toss them on the sink and take out the bottle of powder. "Too messy."

Next is a box of Norforms. "Hmm." Clicking my tongue, I read until my eyes catch the words "melts when inserted." *Trash can!* Wouldn't that be fun? Melting goo dripping out on the man!

One by one, the products get separated out between the trash and the counter. *Finally,* the lotion, something simple and familiar to me. With a spurt to my palm I massage it down my leg…and we hit a snag. My senses are assaulted with the pungent odor of fake jasmine flower.

Are you kidding me? Spooling toilet paper around my hands, I scrub my leg, removing as much of the offending lotion as possible, then grab my loofah and scrub harder. Bent forward, I sniff my leg, satisfied when only a trace of cheap jasmine remains. Good enough.

Hunched down, chastising my drastic behavior, I notice my toes, or more accurately, my toe polish, is a hot mess, chipped and bright blue. No, no, no! What was I thinking?

Everything possibly located in the bathroom goes flying as I manically dig for polish remover, cotton…do I have time for this? I fumble back, resting on the floor. No, nor do I have nail polish.

Breathe in and let it out. I replay the instructions for calming I learned in the one yoga class I took last year. It works… a little. Okay, he won't notice my toes, I tell myself. Why would he when he has all my other body parts revealed and at his perusal?

I stand on wobbly legs and leave the steamy room to search for a *loose* blouse; I'll sweat through it the second I walk in the office otherwise. Once the billowy light blouse is in hand, I scour the closet for pants with no fussy buttons as well as pretty panties and a matching bra.

You know the rule, 'never leave the house in your "that time of the month" granny panties'. The minute you do… you'll find yourself in a car wreck…or in a gyno's office.

By the time I've reapplied deodorant, blotted the clumps, and sprayed perfume up and down my body, including down south, I'm exhausted. Turns out Cherry Almond doesn't mix well with Ocean Spray; my gag reflex hits and I race back into the bathroom and start scrubbing. Now I'll be red and irritated, *freaking fabulous!*

That's it, enough! My hands fly up into my hair, the one thing I could care less about and have done nothing with. This's going from bad to worse to…painful. I grab my cell, finger ready to dial and cancel, when I see the text.

Brady: Don't forget your appt. @10!

I realize all doctors take that darn oath thing, swearing to help all at any time able, but he's a bit too worried about my hooha's health.

Me: On my way out the door

THERE ARE PHONES that unlock with only the owner's thumbprint. They can take a heart out of one body and minutes later, place it in the chest of another, beating new life. People speak live, continents apart, over the internet. And yet no one has mastered the craftsmanship of the "doctor visit robe" beyond crinkly paper with one big ass side open…*unbelievable.*

The unpleasant hint of sweat building in the crease between thigh and ass cheek, as well as the backs of my knees, curtails my focus off the overly detailed illustrations on the walls. I'm left jumping up to shimmy across the cold floor with my ass hanging out to rip some paper towels out of the holder.

Wiping frantically, I dip a hand in my purse and spritz one more time, another scent—it's like Fruitopia down there. *Jesus, just kill me already.*

I'm climbing back on the table, the paper cover over it, in collaboration with my robe, making the loudest crinkling sound possible when a knock on the door spins me around with a startled yelp.

"C-come in," I stammer, straightening myself quickly.

Dr. Reynolds' head peeks around the door, his face lit up with a beautiful, comfortable smile. "Addison, you ready?"

No! "Yes." I manage a brave face for him.

Chapter Four

THE DOCTOR steps in, so young yet so dignified, and closes the door behind him. "How're you today?"

My pulse is rapid, throat dry, skin prickling. "Fine." The simple word hooks in my throat; bad start, try again. Mustering all the bravado I can find, I tear my gaze away from my clammy hands up to meet his. "Fine," I repeat clearer. "You?"

"No complaints." His eyes friendly and shining. "It's probably the best morning I've had in a while."

"Really. That interesting, huh?" I ask, gnawing my bottom lip.

Chart in hand, he hums affirmatively and strolls across the room. "Delivered healthy twin boys to a couple that spent almost a decade trying to conceive. Mama spent half the pregnancy on bed rest." He throws his leg over and straddles the rolling stool. "There's nothing like handing a parent their child for the first time. It's beyond incredible."

Gone are my nerves, replaced with a swell in my heart. "I bet it feels amazing to give them that."

His eyes rise to mine. "Not gonna lie, it feels pretty good." A soft puff of laughter bubbles up at his honesty, releasing the tension from my shoulders as my head tilts down.

All calmness working its way through me vanishes the instant I once again raise my head. He's watching me intently, his eyes holding mine in a commanding grip. The silence hanging over us is no longer natural and easy, but heavy, almost deafening. Goosebumps flare up my legs as the air charges with some foreign electric surge that shivers down my spine and pools in my gut.

It's Dr. Reynolds that breaks the heated connection, dropping his focus to my chart. "First visit, nervous?"

Am I nervous? I'm a lot of things right now, many yet

to be named. I blink twice and subtly shake my head, attempting to brush off the fact that my body's on high alert, eager to discover what exactly just happened between us; that look, that spark.

Does he look at all his patients like that? Better yet, who's *ever* looked at *me* like that?

Whatever it was, it's dissipated, along with my poise, as I watch him read through the forms I filled out in the waiting room. Basic information, but still a reminder of why I'm here and what's about to happen.

Releasing my bottom lip from my teeth, I manage a shaky smile, grateful for his understanding. "Yeah," I breathe out, finally answering him.

He chuckles lightly and pats my knee. "Don't be, you're gonna be fine."

With a curt nod and tightness to my lips, I ready myself.

"So," he clears his throat and glances from me to the chart, "I'd say we'll do your annual, but since you've not been doing that, I guess we'll do your first annual today." He smirks my way at his joke and pulls a pen from his pocket.

His thumb covers the end and the clicking sound it makes sends a shudder straight through me, an obviously visible one considering his handsome face stiffens with a frown.

He wheels closer, that soft, concerned hand finding my knee again. "Addison, please try to relax for me. Would you feel better if I had a female nurse join us?"

An audience?

"No, no." My head shakes rapidly back and forth. "I'm fine, really."

"Yeah?" His eyes search mine. "You sure?" Not sure what I do to tell him yes, but he seems satisfied. "Okay, let's start with some questions. Any concerns or issues you'd like to discuss today?"

"No, I'm only here to avoid a lecture." Though I'm still debating if it's worth all this.

His lip quirks in the corner. "I won't make you sit through another one then, since you're here, but I have to ask. Your paperwork says you've *never* had your Well-Woman Check. Is that an *actual* never, or an 'it's been so long, it was only once, that you just put that' kind of thing?"

"That'd be a never, as in never, kind of thing," I mumble, glancing away.

He slips his stethoscope from around his neck and rolls to the left, centering himself in front of my legs, which are smashed together in terror. "Well, you're remedying it now, and the rest of the information you filled out looks good. So, no other concerns? Regular periods?"

"Yep," I reply tightly.

"Do you give yourself regular breast exams?"

"Um…"

"It's important that you do so."

"Got it," I mumble after a pause, staring at his chest. Not because it's broad and fighting to escape his light blue button up, or even because the open collar hints at a sprinkling of dark brown hair, no, I'm solely transfixed on him rubbing the stethoscope's face there to warm it up.

"Good." He stands, securing the instrument in both ears, then places both hands on the sides of my throat. I startle, twitching a bit beneath his touch.

"Relax, I'm simply checking your lymph nodes."

His face moves closer to mine, his minty breath all I can smell, and then it hits me. My mouth clamps shut, in case mine isn't as minty fresh. *All the crap I sprayed and I forgot about my breath?*

Great, I'm a mute until he backs up at least. No way am I risking it.

"Deep breaths," he says softly, resting one hand on my back, the other placing the instrument to my chest. "Good, again."

I'm confident he can hear my erratic heartbeat. The beating only grows wilder thinking about it and my cheeks flush. The harder I attempt to school my labored breathing, steady my racing heart, the worse it seems to get.

"Addison," he pulls back to look at me, his brow furrowed, "please, try to calm down for me. Would you like a glass of water maybe?"

My shoulders slump on a sigh, aware that I'm being ridiculous. I'm a grown woman, nothing special or different about my anatomy, but Dr. Reynolds is surprisingly attractive. Coupled with the sweet understanding in his eyes, such a gentle touch, and positively virile cologne— this appointment suddenly contains a whole other category of nerve-inducing factors.

I'd flush crimson and breathe rapidly if a hot guy

approached me in a grocery store, let alone one about to get up close and personal with my vagina.

Inhaling a steady breath through the nostrils and out, again through the nostrils only, I ease myself into a place of calmness. For how long, it's hard to tell.

"I'm sorry, I'm fine." I offer reassurance. "Carry on."

"Alright, deep breath again for me." He listens on my back and I use his instructions to settle myself further with each inhale. "Sounds good, now go ahead and lie down."

"L-lie down?" I croak as he makes a note on my chart. Is this it? Have we reached the vagina inspecting stage already?

"Uh huh," he hums in answer, concentrating on his writing.

My stomach rolls and knots as I reluctantly settle my back against the less than durable paper. My chest constricting, eyes bulging. *Shit! Shit! Shit!* My body is about to implode from the coil sprung so tight within me.

"Okay." He's up again moving towards me rubbing his large hands together.

With considerately warmed fingers, he gently grips the top of my robe and starts to pull it open. I must squeak out loud and not just in my head because he stills, looking directly in my eyes.

"I have to uncover your breasts to examine them."

My hands shoot up, clutching the robe shut. "Right, I know, but I forgot I did an exam this morning, myself. They're good, great actually. Two of 'em, exactly where they should be. Round and everything, I swear."

His cheeks redden as he fights a chuckle. "Medicine's come a long way. We check for a bit more than that now." He winks and my coil tightens in deeper places. "I need to make sure there's no suspicious tissue activity or formation. You didn't answer me clearly on whether you did regular breast exams on yourself before. When did you honestly do your last?"

Sneaky bastard—distracting me so I don't notice my grip slackening or the fact that he's uncovered my chest until the cold air hits my exposed nipples. *Of course they harden to a tight bud. Please* tell me all women's do that at this part.

My focus is broken by the low hiss I hear. Was that me or…him?

Definitely him. *Oh God, what?*

"Nothing, everything's fine," his hoarse voice answers the question I didn't realize I'd asked aloud. "Arm up." He helps guide the limb above my head and then...places his fingers to the sensitive flesh of my left breast and begins to knead it, molding it in his skilled hands.

My eyelids slip shut on their own and I snap them back open instantly. *He's a doctor, it's an exam, nothing more.*

Maybe I should have considered having sex last night to prepare for today. With who I have no idea, but it may be of help right now. I squeeze my legs shut in mortification at the fact that arousal is ripping through my every fiber and sweltering in the paper robe.

Focus. Don't squirm. Hell, don't move or blink. Think natural, casual. The expression I muster of "this is totally natural for me" causes his mouth to tug up at the corners. *Am I amusing him?*

I'm crazy and completely overthinking this. I stare up at the ceiling. Could the lights in here be any brighter? It's like being at the dentist, except my dentist is old and bald and smells like Ben-Gay.

Now I admit, albeit embarrassed, I'd be lying if I said it didn't feel odd, yet...*good* to have a feral-smelling, successful, gorgeous man groping—even medically—my breasts. But I don't think I just imagined that. I could swear his fingertips trailed across, never losing contact, as he moved to the right one.

Which maybe that's normal, perhaps they check for something in between them? Didn't feel like that though, felt...teasing.

"And this arm," he mumbles, voice deeper, once again moving it up for me. "Good, perfect."

I finally manage the courage to steal a glance at him, his eyes clearly "examining" as well.

"It's, uh, cold in here." *Now why did I say that?* Maybe he hadn't noticed the perky, aching points shining like headlights, and I just had to go and point it out.

"Too cold?" His hands still with concern and my entire body aches for them to continue. For them to do their best, and worst, to my neglected breasts.

"No," I fumble through embarrassment. "It's—"

"Totally natural." He lifts his gaze to mine and smiles thoughtfully. "All done."

With the gentlest touch I've ever felt, he lowers my arms and places them at my sides. Whether professional or not, I don't complain when he rubs his hands up and down my forearms twice, warming away the chill.

It's tender and innocent, but I can't shake the feeling that it's not his usual protocol. Chivalrously, he offers his hand to help me sit up. "That wasn't so bad, was it? You did excellent and everything felt good," throat clear, "normal," he clarifies, stepping away and swiping the chart off the counter in a rushed maneuver, writing feverishly with his head down.

As the seconds stretch on, I begin to loosen up. The nagging tingle in my stomach releases enough that I can breathe evenly now. He may do this every day with young, old, fat, thin, ugly, and pretty women, but much like I can't stop my nipples from perking up for cold air, he can't help that he is a man groping boobs. We're both but human beings here. My shoulders drop with the easing thought that he too seems a bit *aware of something.*

Finally, he looks up as he retakes his seat on the stool and rolls over to sit before me, front and center. "Next, we need to do a pap smear. I'll take a swab and we send that off to the lab. It tests cervical cells for various cancers or precursors. We usually have the results back in a week.

Now, before your eyes get any bigger, let me just say, it's invasive, but not painful."

Good to know. Still, the stressed breathing has returned, along with the beads of sweat forming down my back.

"You shouldn't have any soreness or discharge afterwards. If you do, call me immediately."

I nod, unsure if he's waiting for me to say the words "I understand" aloud. With the way he's staring at me, it's as if I'm before some judge. I'd think he was nervous himself if he didn't do this daily, hourly. He's simply looking out for his patient like any doctor would. That's evident when he places his hand over mine, locked on the side of the table in a death grip.

"Are you *sure* you don't want a nurse in here? A lot of women do. I completely understand."

His thumb travels over my knuckles and I release my hold on the table.

"How long does it take?" I ask, anxiety evident.

"Two, maybe three, minutes."

"I'm fine then."

"Okay, lie back for me and put your feet in the

stirrups."

"I'm not stirred up! I was actually beginning to feel calmer," I snap, swinging my arms over my chest. *How dare he!*

This time he's unable to contain his laughter, turning away as if I can't hear it. "*Stirrups*," he reiterates through the chuckle. "When raised and locked in place, you put your feet in them." He turns back, laughter gone, but his expression still amused as he points to the medieval looking thingies folded at the end of the table. "Thank you for that though. Days get long without a laugh or two."

Mortification doesn't begin to describe my emotions at the moment. "You can't repeat that, right? Funny water cooler story. There's confidentiality and all, isn't there?" I scowl, not wanting to be the running gyno meetings joke.

All traces of humor vanish instantly. "Addison, I will never," he locks solemn eyes with me, "ever repeat anything that happens in here."

I believe him. "Thank you," I concede, unfolding my arms.

"You ready?"

I sigh and lay back. "As I'll ever be."

The metal clanks noisily as he prepares the stirrups. I tilt my head and watch as he moves a tray and lamp to his side.

"Feet up." He taps my left ankle and helps guide it into the contraption, then does the same with the right. "Now scoot your bottom all the way down."

I do, squirming awkwardly.

"More."

I do so again, the paper robe rustling louder.

He snickers. "A little more."

For Christ's sake. In one big scoot, I'm now as far down the table as I can go before my ass smacks him in the face. He doesn't seem to mind, the opposite in fact.

"There ya go, good." He reaches up and adjusts the neck of the lamp, then puts on gloves, the "pop" echoing off the walls of this ever-shrinking room. "Here we go," he breathes out, opening the robe and fully exposing me.

I groan in embarrassment, louder than I intended, obscuring something that he said. "What?" I ask for clarification.

"I didn't say anything." He's still mumbling.

I close my eyes, trying to hide, but they snap back

open the instant I feel his muscular hands on the inside of my knees.

"Little wider for me," he says softly, gently pushing my tense legs further apart. "Just like that."

Extremely confused by the flaring within me, I grimace to myself and close my eyes once more. I'm undeniably turned on by Dr. Gorgeous' bedside manner, bedside voice, bedside touch. *How sick is that?*

Turned on? Oh God, can he tell? Well, of course now that I wonder if I'm...moist...I instantly feel like I'm gushing, or maybe it's the heat of the lamp? *Please let it be the heat!*

My attempt to bend my legs instinctually is thwarted by his hands, immediately there. "Stay open for me."

Stay open? Is this really happening right now? Yeah, I'm open all right and damn, do I feel it. I turn my head and squeeze my eyes shut as tight as they'll go, silently counting the seconds and willing my body not to react.

"And speculum in," he says an instant before I feel something hard and cold slide inside me, causing me to wince and stiffen. "Easy." He rubs one calf. "Tell me when you're settled."

When I move out of his town.

"Addison?" He peers up at me.

"Yeah, okay, ready." I suck in a deep breath, blowing it out slowly. Almost done, I chant mentally.

"Little pinch," he lies, doing something that's uncomfortable as hell. "Try not to move. I'm going to swab and then we'll be done. You're doing great."

"Uh huh." My voice sounds shaky even to my own ears.

"So did you want to go over anything else today?" he asks, striking up a conversation I could've done without. "Any blood work for communicable testing or birth control?"

"Nope, good on both, thanks." I thought he said two or three minutes. Feels like hours have passed.

"You're good on birth control?" He glances up again, rising slightly to see my face. "I didn't read that in your chart?"

Eyes on the prize, Doc, let's get this done!

"No need. Same with the blood work. I'm fine, trust me," I grumble out the last part. Nosy fucker, outing me as a pathetic, no sex life loser under the guise of medicine.

"Oh, alright then. Well, if that changes, give the office a call and we'll get you in. You need—"

"Twenty-six years old, Doc, I got it!" I cut him off.

He laughs, slowly easing the speculum, I think he called it, out of me. "Almost done, I need to check the positioning of your ovaries and uterus." He stands now, looking down at me. "This will be my fingers in you, Addison."

Fingers? I swallow the lump building in my throat. I'm not sure the breezed over "invasive" warning covers it. I shock myself, having to stifle a giggle with the sudden realization; Dr. Reynolds has literally fingered most of the women in this town.

Oh dear God, who's my mother's gyno? No, no, no. I shake my head...happy thoughts.

I tremble when he touches me, the slow, steady hands of a professional, yet still I twitch. It's the nerves, not excitement, I swear it.

"Relax," he eases with a low voice as one hand covers my stomach, pushing down on my tummy while the fingers of the other slip inside me, both working together to knead and feel around. "You okay?" he asks, me probably

49

mistaking his concern for huskiness.

"Fine," I respond with my eyes closed tight.

"We're all done." He slides his fingers out, turning away abruptly. "You can put your legs down and sit up."

His back remains to me, unlike the reassuring manner before.

"I'm done for a year, right?" I fumble with the damn joke of a robe, covering what I can as fast as possible.

"With that part, yes. Unless you have any changes in life or health, or any questions, you should be good for a year." He's done charting, labeling, and washing his hands and I'm still staring at his broad muscular back straining against his shirt. "You should get your results in a week. I'll step out, you go ahead and get dressed and stop at the front before you leave. Anything else?"

Irritation digs at me that he's keeping his back to me, bordering on rude at this point.

"No, thank you." I manage as graciously as my annoyance will allow.

"My pleasure." He shifts only his head to respond cryptically before promptly walking out.

Chapter Five

HAVE YOU EVER walked from one point to another and upon arrival, weren't exactly sure how you got there? No memory of passing your favorite café or staring idly at the newest selection of overpriced dresses in a boutique's window, your feet merely guiding you off memory alone? That's me this morning.

I left Dr. Reynolds' office in a haze of incoherent ramblings to the receptionist and somehow made it the few blocks to work, my head a fury of mixed emotions and piercing conclusions of what my body had wanted. All I know is that I'm finally here in the tiny break room, slipping off my coat, my exhilarated skin still tingling from his touch.

With a heavy sigh, I head out front. I thought, *ten o'clock appointment, love my job, it'll be fine.* Wrong. I definitely should've taken the entire day off. I never take time off work, but I also never go to gyno appointments, especially ones like *that*, so I had no idea how to plan. Now I wish I had gone straight home after.

"Um…my bad. You okay?" someone asks as I settle in at the computer, eager to check in the next animal and forget everything else.

"What? I'm perfect." I glance up to find it's one of the interns that comes in for school work credits.

She's new, which makes it odd that she's asking me if I'm alright, not to mention staring at me, the beginnings of a mocking grin on her face as though she's about to split open with laughter. My brows pinch, perplexed, that is, until I follow her gaze down to the seat I'm currently occupying.

Slowly, and I mean torturously so, I stand, suddenly aware of the slimy feeling under my ass. Unable to avoid the balks of laughter from not only my coworkers but half the waiting room occupants, I chuckle along, silently berating myself for allowing a man to space me out so much that I just sat on a pudding cup. It's completely squashed under me, since I sat down, oblivious, and now my ass is covered in it. Chocolate, I assume, the only flavor I'm aware of that comes in such a lovely shade of brown…on my ass.

By the end of the day, after changing into the extra pair of scrubs I keep in my locker, in case of an animal mishap, *not my own*, I'm exhausted, and also particularly tired of the new nickname, "Snack Pack." On top of that, I'm flustered and confused, which is evident in my unnatural, shabby quality of work. All I can manage is the motions, my mind a million miles away, replaying and analyzing every single second of this morning.

Is he that gentle with all his patients? Did I imagine the change in timbre of his voice, the low grunts, the hiss I thought joined mine? And why wouldn't he turn and face me when he was done?

The circling clouds of thoughts still plague me when Mimi hears the clock chime and screeches out, "Five o'clock, closing time!"

Couldn't have come a second sooner. I hurry to shut down my computer, grab my things, and rush out the door after some quick goodbyes. Let someone else close up shop tonight—I need some wine and alone time.

Opting for mellow tunes on the ride home, I open the sun roof, in desperate need of a cool breeze on my overheated skin. It's been far too long since I've relished in a man's touch, exam or otherwise, thus my current sweltering and easy dismissal of blood work or birth control. That peace of mind is nice and all, but the flip side is that I'm all worked up. There's a fantasy in my mind and a hunger throbbing in my nether region that both need some attention. All that paranoia that the unbelievable need building between my legs was going to leave me with an embarrassing wet spot haunted me most the day, one of the only things I *was* conscious of.

Finally safe inside my door, I toss down my stuff, not caring where it lands, and kick off my shoes. Wine first! I take the first sip of some crisp Arbor Mist and sigh. Yes, I'm a wine slummer, no fancy-ass smells like Easter egg dye stuff for this girl. My phone alerts me to a text, which I'm tempted to ignore, but my conscience kicks in—they may need help closing the clinic with my mad dash outta there, so I drag myself to retrieve it.

Brady: just checking on ya.

Not about to answer, "I'm horny and on edge," I toss the phone back down. Why even bother with pointless lies?

Anxiety riddling my nerves, I sludge across the apartment. Searching for any sort of relief available, I step in my bedroom, setting the wine on my nightstand and flipping on the ceiling fan. Despite the swirl of coolness in the air, it does nothing to chill my searing body heat.

In a huff of fury, irritated that my mind is fluttering with images of Dr. Reynolds between my legs and hindering my chances of cooling off, I begin to peel off my clothes piece by piece, teasing myself with a slow strip, imagining him whispering "show me," in my ear. All the way down to lingerie, I'm fine, but when my bra hits the floor and my nipples familiarly pebble from the breeze, I'm instantly back *there*. Uncovered, exposed, nervous but tingling, his large, muscular hands exploring me.

"I have to uncover your breasts."

His rich tone plays in my head as my own hands creep up to my heavy, aching peaks, mimicking his movements.

Scenario in my head, I add what I wish he'd done and tug on my nipples, the force pulling all the way to my core. I fall back on my bed with a deep sigh, picturing him giving me the sensations I feel, begging me with his eyes for more.

"I will never repeat what happens in here.

It's almost real, *him* sliding down my panties now, slowly, kissing along their path, a low hum in approval of what he sees. Then—

Then the damn phone's screeching ring shatters my musing. I lay still, panting and naked, waiting for voice mail to pick up. *Ah, silence.* I squeeze my eyes shut and let my hand sneak down my stomach, one finger finding my weeping center, the other hand caressing my breast.

"This will be my fingers in you, Addison."

"God, yes," I moan, pressing my head back into the pillow, stroking my finger in and out of myself seductively slow. My tongue darts out, moistening my lips, lips that crave to taste his, to travel over his neck, down his hard chest. I run my nose through his dark brown happy trail, light hairs smelling of man tickling as my lips kiss their way down to give *him* a special exam.

"Little wider for me."

I bend my legs up, feet flat against the sheets and let my knees fall wantonly open to the side…as wide and willing for him as I can be.

Surely this is some joke. The fucking phone trills out again. I try to ignore it, speeding up the finger inside me, slick and seeking explosion. Someone's overly persistent and calling AGAIN, and my erotic mood's officially stolen away. Even more frustrated now, which I wouldn't have thought possible, I stomp, naked and soaking wet, to grab the damn phone.

"Hello?" I bark without even checking the ID.

"Moe? You okay?"

I release an exasperated stream of air. "Yes, Brady, I'm fine. I would've texted you later, jeez. Ever think I might be busy?" A deaf person would pick up the aggravation in my voice right now.

"I only wanted to check on you but you didn't answer my text or call," he says, sweet concern lacing his voice. "I got worried, that's all."

Well shit. I sigh heavily, feeling bad. "I know, I'm sorry. Helluva day. I'm dying for a long shower and an early night with a good book. I'll talk to you later, okay?"

There's a pause, and then he softly replies. "Okay. Call if you need me. Anything and I'm there." With that he hangs up and I slump back into my sofa.

THE "MOOD" VANISHED, I take an extended cold shower, slip on some light pajamas, and fall asleep by the third chapter of the new action-thriller topping the charts. Normally, I prefer a steamy romance, but opted not to torture myself further.

When I wake in the morning, I'm even crankier and exceptionally aware of my lack of release. Thanks to the vivid, vocal dreams, I tossed and turned through the night; so much for the book theory.

At least it's Thursday. Close to the end of the work week, Tiko night, *and* a morning I have time to head to the gym. That's always a way of boosting endorphins, as though I need more.

I skim through a shower, since there's another one coming up after my workout anyway, and pull my long, dark brown hair in a high ponytail. Bag in hand, dressed to work it hard today, I'm out the door fifteen minutes later.

The drive to the gym is a short one and the lot is close to empty at this time of the morning. I swipe my card and head to the ladies' locker room to put away my bag before I head to the floor. Turning the corner, hurrying to snag my favorite treadmill in front of the TV, I smack into the hard chest of Percy, my favorite To the Max employee.

"Sorry, Addison," he tries for an apologetic grin, "are you alright?"

"Fine," I toss a hand in dismissal and snicker, "since I ran in to you. How are you?"

Percy's always been nothing but a cheerful, helpful gentleman to me, despite Brady's blatant hatred toward him, but this morning something is off. He sighs heavily and glances away, then back to me timidly, as though having to talk to me is killing him. "Crap," he mutters, scrubbing a hand down his face. "Not sure what to do here. It's my business, job and all, but maybe not in the way where I should tell you, but you seem like such a nice person, and—"

"Percy," I place a hand on his arm, hoping to ease whatever's so obviously bothering him to the point of distraught rambling, "what is it?"

"Your boyfriend," he growls.

A relieved chuckle pops out. "I wasn't aware I had one of those."

"Brady? Your boyfriend?"

I shake my head and offer him a reassuring grin. "Not even close, just a good friend. So quit worrying." But... "Why, what'd he do?"

"Oh thank God," his whole body goes lax, "well sorta. I could have sworn you two were an item and I had no clue how I was gonna tell you he's *occupied* with the new blonde, uh, *female* member in the men's locker room. Some sounds are unmistakable, you know?" He blushes fiercely, such a gentleman. "But I still have to decide whether or not I should revoke their memberships."

As disgusted as I am, years of friendship won't allow me not to protect Brady, even when he's not looking.

"Percy," I bat my eyelashes shamefully, "how about I make you a big batch of my signature chocolate peanut butter cup cookies next week, *and* promise to make sure Brady doesn't do this again, and we forget this ever happened?"

His brow cocks. "A batch? How many cookies we

talkin'? I'm a growing boy, ya know." He teases jovially, turning to walk away, motioning with his head for me to follow.

———————— ⌇ ————————

"HEY, GRUMPY, feeling better today?" Brady teases, his twinkling green eyes matching his playful tone as he strolls out of the locker room.

He's standing in front of me but all I can see are his grey tennis shoes since I'm bent in half stretching to my toes. Slowly I raise up, eyes widening as I take him in.

"What," I point, biting down on a giggle, "the *hell* are you wearing? Those shorts could be seen from Mars."

It seems like I was miffed at him for something, but I'll be damned if I can remember now amidst the hilarity before me. Brady is prancing around the gym in neon green shorts at least one size too small. I was there when he bought them; I even tried to warn him they were nothing but an eyesore he'd never wear, but as always, he was more concerned with the perky salesgirl holding them right up against his crotch explaining they were made for him. At that point, I'd retreated to the opposite side of the store, unable to stomach their interaction. That was five years ago and not only have the shorts been collecting dust in his drawer since then, the "oh so sweet girl" turned out to be a raving stalker that enjoyed slashing tires.

The fact that he'd resort to this public display before doing an actual load of laundry is unbelievable…almost as much as the fact he got someone to screw him on the same day as this fashion statement. *Oh yeah, that's why I'm mad at him!*

"Uh huh, you have no idea why I might be wearing these?" He cocks one brow in question.

"Why, whatever do you mean?" I lay on a southern drawl and my best innocent eyes.

"Kathy disappeared this week, no call, won't answer mine. Doesn't sound like her, does it?" He's gauging me intently, waiting for a slip, but I stand firm, nonchalant in my composure.

"I'm sure she'll be back. Probably just needed a break. Anyway," I jab a finger in his chest, "you need to get laid in private! If you get us kicked out of the only gym in town, I'll kill you. You're welcome, by the way; you may repay me by buying all the ingredients needed for two batches of my cookies."

"ChocoPeanaCups?" he says excitedly, his eyes lighting up. "You making those for me?"

"No, Percy. That's how I saved your membership. The locker room? Seriously, Brady?"

"Fucking punk, running to tattle to you. I knew I hated him."

"He didn't *want* to tell me! And so not the point."

His mouth takes on a sinister snark as he leans in, inches from my face. "Oh, he wanted to tell you, believe me... 'Brady's getting in some panties, so please, Addison, finally let me get in yours,'" he mimics. "Limp dick," he mutters with a head shake. "Pathetic."

"Whatever, just keep it in your pants," I glance over him with a smirk, "or groovy shorts, at the gym. Promise?"

"Yeah, yeah," he blows me off, so I do the same.

"Run along now," I shoo him with my hand. "I've got a workout to get to."

To my delight, my favorite treadmill is still empty. I pop in my headphones and start at a steady pace. Blah. CNN's on the TV in front of me, so I turn to the second best form of entertainment—people watching. The key to good creeping is subtlety. Never let them catch you looking. I've mastered it, which is why Brady has no clue that I'm currently rolling my eyes and fighting back a sudden case of heartburn as I spy on him now shamelessly flirting with a redhead with airbags for breasts. He literally *just* finished getting laid; the man never quits.

Not surprised, though, Ginger's totally his type…she appears to be breathing and has huge tits. Despite myself, an intruding thought crosses my mind. I wonder if Dr. Reynolds is *her* gyno? He'd have a field day with her breast exam.

I glance down to my own set, not bad, big C's, still high and proud. And real. So real in fact, I wince and slow down my speed as they bounce up to tell me I forgot to grab the good sports bra this morning.

Brady's now caught my gaze from across the room and is walking toward me. Geez, did I not shoo him away only minutes ago? Miss Thing's mouth is still moving, probably offering 69 different positions to coerce him to stay, but he ignores her, dead set on his path to me.

Bitch gives me a dirty look, *please,* if I had a dollar for every one of Brady's thwarted toys that saw me as a threat, I could open my own *private* gym.

He gently tugs out my earbuds. "Your ass and legs are fine. Wanna work on arms? I'll spot ya?" he asks, his voice chipper.

"Did you just compliment my ass and legs or insult my arms? I can't decide. And it looked like you were kinda busy not working out." I huff all that, never breaking my stride. "Then again, I guess you did already get a workout this morning with a different girl."

"Yeah, but not with my *favorite* girl, though, so here I am." He climbs on behind me, keeping pace, very close to my back.

"Brady! There can't be two people on here. Stop," I complain, pouting, "before you really do get us kicked out. And back up off me, did you even shower after initiating the new member?" I gag.

"Of course I did! I'm the cleanest son of a bitch you know, despite my current lack off such dishes or underwear. Now admit you're behind Kathy's disappearance and I'll get down," he whispers, gusts of exerted air on my neck.

Of all the things that transpired already this morning, this is what he's focused on. More than sure he'll seek revenge at some point, perhaps a simple confession will lesson his retaliation later. It's worth a try, at least. "Promise you won't make any more appointments for me and I'll think about it."

His fingers trail delicately down my back and settle on my hip, eliciting a shudder that I struggle to hide. I'm too on edge to deal with any male contact, even Brady's.

"Hands off! Just because the redhead got you all worked up, doesn't mean you get to cop a feel on me!" I chastise a little meaner than necessary, scooting up, away from his grip.

His tone is unaffected by my reprimand. "I promise, for at least a year anyway, to not make any more appointments for you. I only did it because I care about you, Moe. It's my job to protect you, especially when you won't do it yourself. It's what people in my profession do. I guarantee you the first thing a fireman does is replace the smoke detectors in his loved ones' homes."

Two strong hands brace around my waist, saving me from a face plant as the roll of the treadmill stops suddenly, Brady having pushed the button with no warning or permission. "Come on," he grabs my hand, "let's do arms."

I follow along, no point in arguing. The benches are on a different floor, one filled with hard-bodied men in tight, or missing, shirts, sweat dripping down their six times *pick a big number* packs as they lift impressive weights. "Get pumped up" music plays overhead...and I appear to be the only female in the vicinity.

"Let's start on this one." He points with one hand, the other on my back, guiding me to an empty bench.

"What's it do? Or what do I do? Never used it before." I stare in nervous wonder, thinking back to a certain medieval contraption.

"Sit straddled on it, facing away, then lie back for me."

Lie back for me.

My body the betrayer. My heartbeat slowly picks up its pace and my face begins to heat as I suppress a moan. The sexy throb of music isn't helping. I do as he says then look up with a small gasp—he's standing above me, his legs straddled on either side of my body.

I can see up the leg of his 80's disco shorts. He really is out of underwear.

"Think you can do sixty pounds?" He eyes the weights deliberately.

"I have no idea, Brady," I admit. "Again, never done it before. But I know I don't want to get hurt or have my chest crushed."

He bends down, his face not a full centimeter from mine, and pushes the sweaty bangs off my forehead. "That's what I'm here for, silly girl. I won't let you get hurt. We'll do fifty."

I watch as he rearranges discs and such onto the bar, the muscles in his nicely toned arms— I'd never tell him that—flexing with every movement. After that appointment yesterday, the reminders today, Brady's decent physique and my drought of…well, anyway, I appear to be having strange, alarming reactions to a man I've known most my life. A man I've seen, while hiding in Dylan's closet, stuff folded socks in his pants before his eighth grade dance.

Of their own, mischievous accord, my eyes drift *there*, scrutinizing. Definitely no socks these days, no room for em'. My stomach tightens, a throb of desire pooling from deep within me as I train my focus anywhere but on him. With all the half-naked men crowding the room, I'm left at the mercy of my ever growing arousal, back with a vengeance at the worst possible time.

Brady lowers the bar and all I can see is his hard, chiseled chest, causing my nipples to pebble and harden. This can't be happening. Not with *Brady*. I need some relief, something to stop me before I fly up and take my sexual frustration out on him. I quake at the thought, my legs trembling, but it does nothing to settle my arousal.

"Moe?" He snares my attention, hint of a tamed laugh in his tone. "You look a little flushed. Distracted? You need a water break?"

"Yes! Water sounds great." I shoot up, ducking the bar, sliding off the bench and around him. "Getting a drink," I yell awkwardly, dashing for the ladies' locker room...and passing two fountains on the way.

Until I figure out my whacked-out emotions and reactions, which I suddenly seem to have no control over, I've gotta get out of here. It seems a beast has been awoken in me and until I find a way to feed it, it'll have to be kept caged, away from the public.

"Mocifus?" Brady calls, rounding the row of lockers to find me gathering up my stuff.

"Did you *read* the membership rules before you signed

them?" I chuckle, more nervous than amused. "No guys in the women's locker room, *or vice versa.*" I cock an insinuating brow.

"Don't give a shit; worried about you. Wanna tell me what's going on in that head of yours?" He moves into my space, our chests so close they nearly brush together as we both breath heavier than usual. It's the workouts, I tell myself. "Was it your appointment yesterday? You need to tell me if something bothered you." He's frowning at me and I can't stand it. I never could bear to see him truly upset.

"No, it's not that, everything was fine. I don't feel great is all. I'll eat before work. That should help." I throw my bag over my shoulder, avoiding his eyes, and make to leave.

His hand on my arm stops me. "Let me carry that. I'll walk you out. You think you feel too bad for Tiko's tonight? Nothing a 'rita and cheese dip can't cure." He winks, almost all signs of concern wiped away as we head out of the locker room.

Brady, Dylan and I have had a long standing Thursday night date at Tiko's since I was old enough to drink. We prep for the upcoming weekend—Fridays rock on their own, so we steal an extra day— with margaritas, Mexican food and gripes about work. Sometimes we throw in some karaoke, depending on how generous they're making the margaritas.

"Not sure." I shrug noncommittally. "We'll see how I feel after work. You two will manage fine without me if not."

"If not what?" my brother asks, appearing out of nowhere, standing in front of us now.

"Dylan?" I shake my head, astonished, perhaps even hallucinating. "You do realize it's seven o'clock in the morning, and this is *a gym*?"

"Funny." He shoves my shoulder, Brady's hand already there to brace me. "He made me." He points and scowls at Brady. "What were you guys talking about?"

"Moe's not feeling well. She may skip tonight," Brady answers for me.

"You okay?" There's the worried brow, the brother I adore shining through. "We can chill at yours if you'd rather? Oh shit, wait," he snaps, a frown setting in, "Brady and I have dates."

"We have what?" Brady asks, obviously unaware of his match-up.

"Yeah, two ER nurse hotties I met when I picked you up the other day. Shawna and…" he thinks a moment, eyes pinched, "Annie! So we probably shouldn't miss it. If you're up to coming, sis, you might want to find a date too, unless you're cool with being fifth wheel?"

Right back to the brother I want to maim. For years, this has been our thing and he just goes and changes it up *and* refers to me, an original founder, as the fifth wheel?

Oh hell no!

"I'll be there." I jut out my chin. "With a date, a *hot* one that will have your girls drooling!"

Brady chuckles behind me, squeezing the arm he never released from catching me earlier. "Come on, I'll walk you out." He turns his head back and shoots off to Dylan, "Try not to lock me into any more blind dates while I'm gone. And no more fucking with the sanctity of Tiko night, man. Not cool."

Chapter Six

T-MINUS EIGHT HOURS to find a date, how hard can that be? Aren't guys always bitching how a woman can wake up and declare, "I'm gonna get laid today" and make it happen, but a man has to wait till *she* decides? So a simple date, preferably a hot one? Piece of cake.

I arrive at work unshowered, my skin crawling with grime because of the slight change of course at the gym. I compensate by spritzing myself with one of my handy new purchases to freshen up and move on. I've pushed all nagging thoughts of Dr. Reynolds, Brady, and stimulating play from my head and am focused on my immediate goals:

work, find a date.

Mimi greets me as I turn on the lights, fire up the computers, and flip on the open sign. Rushing through morning feedings, I feel bad shortening some of the ear rubs, but I've got to make extra time for my date search.

Finishing up and still the only one here, I consult the contact list in my phone. Eleven males. Eleven, which isn't exactly a self-esteem boosting number. And of those one is Brady, five more are actual relatives, two are now married, and one is…yep, he died last year.

Of the remaining three, I'd tried to date two…delete both.

Last one—Dr. Reynolds' office.

Alrighty then, plan B it is. I quickly fire up Facebook, searching madly though my friends list. I don't know half these people, some of whom no one knows, because they're not real people. Scznyi Axyzges wants to be your friend? Can't date a guy whose name I can't pronounce or lives a continent away, can I?

Nevermind.

My forehead drops pitifully onto the desk, rethinking the fake stomach virus ploy. Who wants me tagging along anyway? Maybe we've outgrown our tradition.

I'm pulled out my self-deprecating lull when my phone beside me dings with a text. One guess who it is.

Brady: Not the same w/out you, Moe. Say the word and it's pizza at yours. Or if you're actually sick, say that, and it's Dr. Me & Patient You. Soup included.

The smile that breaks across my face is uncontainable.

Me: I'll be there @ 7

Brady: Then so will I

Going stag doesn't bother me now. I'm not the odd duck, the newbie, the outsider—their dates are. I'll be back next week. Them? Chances are slim to none.

When four o'clock rolls around and no date is in sight, I'm okay with it. I'm gently getting "Bruiser," a small poodle whose leg got casted today, settled in a cage when in walks Ricky, followed closely by a yellow mop bucket he's towing.

"Hey, Addison, how ya been?"

Once the dog's situated, I close the cage and stand, greeting him somewhat uncomfortably. "Good, you?"

Ricky's not at all ugly, he's quite attractive, in fact, with striking blue eyes, golden skin, a nice physique and mussed blond hair. He's everything most girls are looking for... until he opens his mouth.

"Fine," he grins lewdly, speaking to my chest. "View's pretty damn good too."

Told ya. Bad idea, Addison, you were just resolved to going stag, keep walking.

"Any big plans for the weekend?" I ask with no idea why. *Friendly, simply being friendly.*

His eyes widen, as shocked by my question as I am. Of the million times he's tried to engage me in conversation, this is the first time I've bitten.

"Dunno, little of this, little of that." He wags his eyebrows suggestively. "Why do you ask, gorgeous?"

Fifth wheel—a very helpful tool used for hauling many an item. Walk. Away.

"I was just curious. What about tonight?" I glance around the room, mentally kicking my own ass. "I usually—"

"Yes."

His quick, firm agreement startles me. "I, uh, didn't tell you—"

"Yes. Whatever it is, I'm in. What time should I pick

you up?" His face beams bright, eyes filled with nothing but pure lust and intrigue.

Is he moving closer? *Easy there, eager beaver.* HIS. Not mine.

"Oh, I'll uh, I'll meet you there," I say stiffly, nerves buzzing into a tittering laugh at myself as I scoot along the wall toward the door. "Tiko's, 7ish. That work?"

"Hell yeah, that works. Plenty of time to finish mopping and get myself all *prepared* for you, doll face."

There's his eyebrow wiggle again. It's a struggle to maintain a straight face and not scrunch my nose at what "preparation" he's thinking. No need for anything special on my account.

"You sure you don't want me to pick you up? I'd love to see where that tight body sleeps at night."

"I'm sure!" I yell over my shoulder, already halfway down the hall. "See you there."

Pervert—yes. Harmless—I'd always believed so. Breathing and purpose serving— mission accomplished. I blow out a breath, hoping I haven't started something I won't be able to avoid after tonight. Last thing I need is an innuendo-fueled stalker on my heels at work every day.

With a date checked off my list, it's a mad dash to get home and ready. I finally take my post-gym shower, although hurried, and throw on an attractive-but-casual ensemble. My hair is long and thick, so I flip my head, hit it for a few minutes with the blower, and leave it down, knowing it'll dry into a nice, natural wave on the way over.

When I arrive at the restaurant, the boys and their dates are already there, at the same table as always, visible through the door. Playing the dutiful date, I decide to wait for Ricky outside so we can walk in together, as though we rode that way.

That simple plan is thrown to the wind, literally, when evening gusts begin to pick up unexpectedly and my pink halter tank is no longer cutting it. The man better hurry the hell up.

It's as this thought passes and I cross my arms in a shiver that he comes striding toward me, looking more than presentable in dark-washed jeans and a black button up, hair combed nicely, freshly shaved besides his usual trimmed goatee.

"Hey sexy, why're you outside? It's freezing." He places his hands on my shoulders and begins to rub them up and down my arms. I go with it, allowing him to treat me like an actual date. "Need me to warm up that fine ass too?"

So close, one sentence too many.

"Thank you but no, let's just go in." I step away from his seeking hands, he can use those to open the door. Waiting too long, I impatiently tsk and pick up his slack, opening the damn thing myself. Great start.

"Señorita!" Juan greets me when we walk in. "You're joining your amigos?"

"Yes." I return his hug. "You're busy, I see them."

Brady's already standing with the chair beside him pulled out when we reach the table, attempting to place me between himself and Ricky. *Thanks, but I'm a big girl.* The sidelong glance I shoot him tells him so, but his sternness isn't budging.

So overprotective. All the men shake hands as I get situated then sit, the silence not allowed to last.

"Hi, I'm Shawna." The date in blue sticks out a hand to me. "You must be Addison, it's nice to meet you."

"Likewise." I smile, trying to school my face for who I assume is my brother's date.

"I'm Pat." The girl directly across from Brady takes her turn. Why did I think it was Annie? Oh well, Pat definitely suits her better.

"Hi, nice to meet you. This is Ricky," I introduce him with warm acknowledgement directed his way. There's no meaning behind it, but again, my mantra tonight is "go with it."

Predicting me as usual, Brady scoots the cheese dip my way. I snare a chip and dig in, unable to resist. I swear they pack this stuff with crack; I could devour the whole bowl, something I've proven on more than one occasion.

Conversation picks up around me as I stuff my face, ignoring Ricky's arm draped across the back of my chair, his thumb occasionally brushing my skin. When I go to pour myself a margarita out of the pitcher in the middle of the table, it's already done, sitting in front of me. I look up, Brady watching me, flashing a "you're welcome" wink.

As Ricky and Dylan go head to head over some new video game sweeping the market, Brady leans in and whispers, "Isn't he your clinic's creepy janitor?"

"Shush, he's cute and…" Yeah, I have no other adjective to describe the man whose hand is now trailing freely over the slope of my shoulders. The urge to sit back in my chair and deny him access is tempting, but I refrain, instead firing back at Brady.

"Aren't your dates *dating?*" I quip with a sarcastic smirk. The two girls are lost in the table discussion but constantly looking at each other. And *Pat*...haven't made a decision on her yet.

"I think so." He chuckles. "But your brother picked them, not me. What's your excuse?" His lighthearted tone deceiving his severe scrutiny cast upon Ricky's hand.

"Right, Addison?" My name catches my attention so I turn to Ricky.

"I'm sorry, what?" I ask, overly kind.

"Shawna and Pat here don't think I can take them in *Mortal Fear.* Tell them how good I am."

"Take them where? And why are they scared?" I've only had a few sips, so why is this conversation completely disturbing?

He laughs animatedly and slaps his hand down over my thigh, a little too high for a first date, and leaves it clamped there, giving a suggestive squeeze. "The game, *Mortal Fear.* The one I always play in the break room?

Aren't I good?"

Ah, because it *is* disturbing. But what's even more so is the way his hand is creeping around to my inner thigh. Before I can make a move to *re*move his hand, I hear the low, undeniable growl emanating from Brady. When I glance his way, his penetrating stare is still locked on Ricky's hand, looking more menacing by the second.

"She has no clue what you're talking about. Moe hates video games. Don't ya, sis?" Dylan challenges me from across the table.

With a hollow laugh, I casually place my hand over Ricky's and weave my fingers through his. The move is too tender for what he deserves, but I'm not giving Brady the satisfaction of seeing me freak out. I asked Ricky to be here and he's just being friendly. Ricky-style friendly.

I turn to the two women and do my best to make cheerful conversation. "So, you play video games?"

They talk excitedly over each other, "oh my God this" and "freaking awesome that," while I plaster on a mask of interest that pains my cheeks as I try to listen, appearing interested.

Then it's all four of them, leaning across the table,

phones out, quoting scores and friending each other on whatever gaming sites while Brady and I lean back and sip our drinks, willing time to race.

Juan approaches the table to take our orders and we're the only two that notice, or know what we want—another pitcher, STAT. Maybe if they forget to order, I can do cheese dip and a buzz and get the hell out of here.

"No way, you have to leave the princess until at least level 10 or your key's unguarded for Zylyn to steal," Pat explains.

Ricky unthreads our fingers and slaps his own forehead, positively beaming with admiration. "Why didn't I think of that?"

Thank Christ! I subtly wipe my hand on the napkin in my lap, ignoring Brady's silent amusement, bouncing shoulders giving him away. Yeah, yeah, so I'm wiping off possible cooties, ha ha.

"That's brilliant!" Dylan speaks loudly, making a note in his phone.

Once I toss the napkin back on the table, I rest my head in my palm. I could be...doing anything else right now. Organizing my cupboards. Cleaning out my refrigerator. Alphabetizing my CDs. It's when Ricky's hand settles back on my upper thigh that I make my decision— date night over. They really may not even notice, four heads leaned together in conspiracy, engrossed in the world of all that is gaming. But still, subtle and graceful is the way to make my exit.

"Oh my God!" I jump up, knocking over my chair. "I, um, I started my period! I have to go!" I grab my purse, avoiding the quizzical stares cast my way only but a moment before they're once again locked in a circle. *Helluva plan Addison, 'cause calmly saying you had to work in the morning wouldn't have been graceful.*

I choked.

Brady's up in a flash too. "I'm a doctor! I'll help." He digs furiously in his jacket pocket, pulling out his wallet and tossing bills on the table. "That's for ours, Dyl, you good?"

Engrossed in What's Her Name's phone, Dylan barely manages a thumbs up.

"Bye, Ricky, sorry, thank you for tonight!" I once again find myself yelling as I walk away from him. A flash of guilt hits, so I pivot, relieving myself immediately of any sense of obligation as I watch Ricky's hand grip and rub the back of Pat's neck. They *so* have my blessing.

"You in your car?" Brady leans in and asks, pushing me to the door by my back as I nod. I pull my keys out and he snares them immediately. "Good, my car's still at work and I only had one drink. I'll drive."

WE LAUGH the entire trip to my place, completely sure no one would believe us if we told them about our night—which we won't.

"You should probably pick your own dates from now on." I snicker at him.

"Yours too apparently. The janitor? You could do so much better, Moe."

"Not everyone's a doctor, Snobby Butt. Being a janitor's the least of my concerns. His pervy comments, *much* bigger problem."

"Fine, pick a reason. You could do better. And that fucking hand of his was a little too friendly for my taste. I was about to teach him some respect."

I have no words, I can only stare at him, jaw dropped. Brady's always been a bit hard on the guys I bring around, but he's never suggested violence before. Both of us out of sorts, it doesn't register, until parked at *my* house...that we're in *my* car.

"We should talk, brilliant duo and all." I laugh and he joins in. "No way I feel like driving all the way to your house then back."

He curtly shakes his head. "Wouldn't let ya anyway, I saw you throw back the drinks. I'll drive home and pick you up in the morning to hit the gym, then you can drop me at work. Cool?"

"Fine," I easily concede, seeing as he's used my car a million times before. "Why's your car still there anyway? They picked you up?"

"Yeah, Dylan and *the dates*."

"And *which* one was your date again?" I bite back my snicker, unable to resist giving him hell.

Stifling a chuckle of his own, he tilts his head and ponders. "I have absolutely no idea."

"I figured. Okay then, great night. See ya in the morning." I smile and climb out, jerking back a bit in shock at how fast he's standing in front of me. "What're you doing?"

"It's late. I'm walking you to your door. Plus, I need to

use your bathroom." He admits sheepishly, busted on the pseudo-chivalry.

The walk to my apartment is nothing new or special but there's *something* different tonight. No, I refuse to over analyze it. The man has pissed in my bathroom more than anyone besides myself. Nothing strange going on. Nothing at all.

The second I have the front door open, Brady flies past me down the hall and I mosey to my bedroom to change. "Lock it when you leave," I holler.

"Huh?"

I jump, holding my nightshirt in front of me when his head pops in. "I said, lock up when you leave."

"Of course." He turns to go, peering back with a devilish twist to his lips. "By the way, when'd you open a drugstore? Lotta girly shit in there for only one girl." He winks and heads out. "Night, Moe, sweet dreams."

I hide my face in my hands even though he's gone and can't see me.

My bathroom, shopping spree, productpalooza....

He saw.

Chapter Seven

INCESSANT RINGING wakes me—*as though Monday mornings aren't dismal enough on their own*—the shrill noise piercing my brain no matter how many times I reach out through the sleepy fog and slap the damn thing.

Probably because it's not my alarm.

Groggily, I fumble around, following the noise of my phone. When I see the name flashing, I'm wide awake—my brother? What's going on with him lately? First his early appearance at the gym, of all places, and now this. Dylan has never been up before noon in his life but suddenly he's pulled it off twice in one week. I'm officially worried.

Something must be wrong to rouse him this early.

"Dylan, what is it? Oh God," I choke through the panic, "are you okay?"

"Rise and shine, Mocifus," he chirps. "You free for lunch today?"

My unsteady breath trips up my words. "W-what?"

"Lunch? You, me, whadda ya say?"

"Dylan, it's seven in the morning! Who's dead? What's on fire?"

He chuckles annoyingly in my ear. "Not a damn thing's wrong, everything's right. Can you meet me? I have big news I wanna tell you about in person."

Oh hell, he knocked someone up. I blanch. As scary as the thought is, maybe it's the kick in the ass he needs to learn some responsibility. Please let the girl be someone I can tolerate for the next twenty years.

"You there?" he asks, full of excitement.

Shame on you, Addison. I shake off my pessimism. "Yeah, ok, lunch is good. When and where?"

We make plans to meet at McAllister's Sports Bar at noon. I love their wings *and* it means I won't be eating in the break room. Ricky joined me there on Friday to "end things" because he and Pat "mesh." *Longest conversation without rolling my eyes and gut laughing ever.* Today's venue is all the motivation I need to drag myself to the coffee pot.

As I get ready for work, random scenarios run through my mind of what Dylan's news could be. I adore my big brother, but he tends to be...flighty. An announcement from him could literally be anything from "I joined the circus" to "I'm getting a sex change."

So yeah, to say I'm a bit on edge would be an understatement.

Nevertheless, when I walk in the pub at noon on the dot, I sport a big, optimistic smile of support.

He waves from his perch at a high-top, beckoning me over, dressed in slacks and *a tie.* The fabric strips men wear around their neck, knot at the top—yeah, that kind of tie.

So maybe not the circus then. So far so good.

"Hey." He stands and hugs me. "Thanks for coming. I ordered those cheese bits you like to start. Here." He pulls out my chair. "Take a load off."

"T-thank you." I glance around, trying to spot the *Punk'd* crew, wherever they're hiding. Never once has Dylan been a gentleman! I'm antsy and my patience is waning, but I try to hold firm waiting for the big news. No way would he dress up to declare he's about to become a father, so I'm at a panicky loss. "Out with it, you're scaring me."

"Ah, ye of little faith." He shakes his head and clicks his tongue. "Ok, are you sitting down?"

"Um, you pulled out my chair," I deadpan. "Guess."

"Right, ok sorry, lil' nervous." His face lights up, eyes brightening as he rubs his hands together furiously. "Here goes. Moe, I'm opening my own company. Game software."

I try for a speedy recovery, schooling my bulging, shocked eyes, snapping my agape mouth closed. "How? I mean, I know you're very passionate about those games," I lay my hand over his, hopefully it softens my words of skepticism, "and you're good at them. But Dylan, it takes a lot more than *Pac-Man* prowess and obsession to own a company."

He pulls his hand away from mine, defensive and hurt, scowling. I hate making him feel that way and I'd love nothing more than to see him succeed at something he enjoys, but I've lent him money and helped him move too many times to not say *something*.

"Dyl, you need a business plan, collateral, a building, equipment, employees to whom you can offer benefit packages." I sigh, my chest tight, taking in the disappointment in his features. "Not to mention customers."

There's fifty more things I could rattle off but it's then that our waitress arrives with drinks and appetizer in tow. I'm grateful for the moment of reprieve.

"Thank you." I look at her, snagging an extra dressing off her tray. "I'm ready to order if…" I turn to Dylan. "You know what you want?"

"Let's wait," he says directly to our waitress. "We're expecting one more."

She nods and retreats as I ask, "Who's joining us?"

"The investor who took care of the building and equipment when I showed him my business plan." He fires back smugly.

"Who would—"

"Hey, sorry I'm late. You guys been here long?"

My head's down, sipping my drink, when the familiar voice hits us. Of course…savior Brady.

"Nah, thanks for coming," Dylan answers him as I look up, staring forward.

"I take it he told you." Brady grabs the chair beside me then leans in to my ear and whispers, "Tell me, do you stay mad just so I'll tell you how fucking cute you look when you pout?" He laughs, only momentarily, as I kick him under the table. His hand disappears to rub his shin, still lightly sniggering. "So, catch me up. What'd I miss?"

"Shit, I should've got a refill while she was here. I can't eat without a drink, hang on," Dylan gets up with his glass and wanders off in search of the waitress. "Don't eat them all, Moe!"

The second he's out of earshot, I turn narrowed eyes on Brady. "So when you let him move in and I said quit enabling him, you took that to mean buy him a company? What the hell, Brady? Things handed to you aren't worth working for! Dylan needs to learn that work is hard and bosses suck, but you do it anyway, until you earn more, because that's what adults do!"

His easy demeanor is gone, replaced with a tight jaw. "And I told you, all he needs is a shot, someone to believe in him, which I do, and it pisses me off that you don't! He has a good business plan, Moe, have you seen it? Have you asked to see it? I don't have money because I go around throwing it away." He pops a cheese bite in his mouth and I'm tempted to reach down his throat and take it back.

"*No*, you have *money* from a pathetic trust fund your dead beat father left you! And once again, I'm the bad guy all because I want stability for *my* brother?" My anger slowly dissolves into hurt, softening the harshness in my tone. "I'm tired of lying to our parents and saying 'he's doing great!' I'm tired of moving him around and checking to see if he's got groceries. And I'm tired of you swooping in to be his hero. What happens when you have a family? You still gonna raise him too?" I prop my elbow on the table and grip my hair, letting out an exasperated sigh.

He smoothly runs his finger over my cheek. "Maybe you're mad because you didn't dream bigger, because you stopped at vet tech, eager to turn a paycheck, scared to go all the way and open your own clinic."

"I like my—" My defensive statement is cut short, silenced when he takes my chin in his hand.

Our eyes meet in a fiery battle. "You think he's helpless, dependent on me? Well you're dependent too,

Moe. That clinic could close tomorrow, do cutbacks, fire you. And guess what? That security you think you have that allows you be so high and mighty?" He shakes his head, eyes never straying from mine, fingers loosening on my chin. "It'd be gone. You'd be crying for help from your loser enabler boy then too."

My gasp comes out louder than I'd hoped, anger, shock, and hurt coursing through me. I rear back out of his grip and stand, overturning my stool. My chin is quivering, pulse racing as I snatch my purse. "Tell Dylan good luck and tell yourself," I take a deep breath, "to fuck off."

With that said, I storm from the restaurant, another lunch break ruined. Make that a whole day ruined.

Hours later and I'm still seething; not so much mad at Dylan as worried about him. But Brady? Steaming mad at that asshole. How dare he talk to me like that? I love my job and I'm damn good at it. And excuse me if yes, an income, my own life, sounded better than years of Ramen and student loans.

I'm still doing what I love, helping animals.

Except today; today I'm scaring them off with the piss poor mood and angry vibes oozing from me. Even Roscoe, a bloodhound too old to lift his own head, has growled at me twice.

I get pulled away from Tabby's hissing to answer an important phone call. *Oh no, it's not a bad joke,* too coincidental to happen anywhere but in a badly written sitcom with canned "oohs" and "ahhs." It's actually happening.

"Hello?"

"Miss Porter, hi, this is Samantha from Dr. Reynolds' office. Sorry to bother you, but we need you to come in for some retesting. Your last results were reported back as inconclusive."

"What does that mean, *inconclusive?*" I look around, making sure none of my coworkers are eavesdropping.

"Miss Porter, I'm not licensed or qualified to discuss that with you. Only Dr. Reynolds can do that, so I need to make you an appointment. Is next Wednesday at one okay for you?"

"*Next* Wednesday? Like not the one in two days, the one in nine?" *Is she kidding me?* You don't drop a bomb on my already war-ravaged battlefield and then tell me I need to wait eons for an explanation. "Uh, no, actually, it's not.

I'm not waiting that long to find out what's wrong with me. I want in as soon as possible, please."

"That is as soon as—"

"Listen, Samantha," I cut her off snidely, which I'll feel guilty for later, "you can't call a woman with evasive, worrisome news like that and then expect her to get any sleep. I need you to go ask Dr. Reynolds when he can fit me in, please."

"Yes, ma'am, please hold."

My boot's tapping and I chew my nails, a habit I quit years ago, as I wait. If this hasn't been an awesome day I don't what has.

My entire body trembles when she returns to the line, snapping me from my spiraling thoughts. "Miss Porter?"

"Yes."

"Dr. Reynolds said to come in at 10 am tomorrow. He'll move things around for you."

I exhale and let my shoulders relax a bit. "Perfect, tell him thank you. I'll be there."

After hanging up with her, of course my first instinct is to call Brady and see what he thinks, so he can tell me the possible meaning, options, etc., but I can't do that, seeing as how only hours ago I told him to fuck off.

Not to mention, that'd be asking for help and he made it perfectly clear he's just waiting for the chance to throw *that* in my face.

No, I'll go home, have some brown-bag wine and a hot bath and face this tomorrow like the independent adult that I am.

"Jennifer," I call to the other tech as I gather my things, "I have to leave for the day and I'll be late tomorrow. I've got an emergency appointment that can't be helped."

She comes in the room, concern lining her eyes and brow. "Is everything okay? Can I do anything?"

"Thanks, Jen, that's sweet of you. Can you hold down the fort here and let the others know?" I smile hopefully. "I'm sure everything will be fine."

Once out of the building, I inhale a lungful of fresh air and trudge straight to my car. I can't drive home fast enough, deadbolting the door, turning on some Miles Davis and opening the wine as I head to the bathtub.

So done with this day.

Maybe I'm delirious with fear about my results or

maybe I'm actually deranged and badly in need of an alignment to my priorities, because in spite of it all, one lingering thought induces a shiver…

I'm headed back to see Dr. Reynolds.

Chapter Eight

AGAIN with the paper robe? Why even pretend? We all know I'm as good as naked minus my favorite pair of smooching frog socks snuggling my toes.

There's no fancy schmancy prep this time; I'm in far too foul a mood. Only a rushed hot shower, one squirt of lavender and a quick leg and pit shave. I did, however, brush my teeth *twice*, now keenly aware he prefers to be up close and personal with more than just my cha-cha.

Other than that, this is as good as it gets.

I spent all night tossing and turning, anxious about my results, mad I'd missed more work, and positively distraught at the current state of affairs with Brady and Dylan.

So when Dr. Reynolds knocks and steps in bearing that charming smile, and dear God wearing the sexiest pair of blue scrubs I've ever seen in my life, I almost feel bad for the scowl I'm throwing back.

"Addison," he regards me, airing on the sign of caution, "how're you?"

"Not great, Doc, not even close. Kinda wanting to speed things along and go straight for a drink. It's gotta be five o'clock somewhere, right?"

He glances around, noticeably uncomfortable, before blowing out a long winded breath. Obviously he was expecting the universally acceptable response of, "fine, how are you?"

Not today, sorry, Doc.

"I, um," he stammers, concentrating on the damn all-knowing chart. "Anything I can do?"

"Ha," I scoff. Doesn't matter—doctors, lawyers, trash men, janitors—they're all still *men*, so they have no clue what to say.

"You could explain my test results. My first ever exam

was nerve-wracking enough. Getting a call that my results are," I air quote, "'inconclusive,' well, it scares the shit out of me, quite frankly."

With that admission, my catty, sniping anger is gone, replaced with a trembling lower lip and watering eyes. "And I couldn't even call my best friend to get a medical opinion on it, because again, quite frankly, he's an asshole."

Another thing all men, any walk of life, have in common—they can't stand it when a woman starts to cry.

Dr. Reynolds rises from the stool and moves to stand directly in front of me. "Hey, shhh." He rubs my knee. "Addison, everything will be fine, I promise."

I wipe my palms down my face, a mess inside and out. "Th-thank you for fitting me in, by the way. I appreciate it." I sniffle, long past simply feeling vulnerable. "I'm sorry, I'm just overwhelmed, worried, exhausted." I wave my hand as though "shooing" away the unbearable list. "Anyways, please, can we just get this over with? I need to know what's going on."

Head ducked to meet my eyes, his empathic smile soothes me. "Inconclusive means just that. Not good, not bad, not anything. Something made it impossible to get any results at all."

That's my vagina all right—never getting any results.

"Addison," he taps the hand still on my knee, bringing me back from thought, "did you by any chance douche before you came in that day?"

Oh dear God, he'd smelt the vinegar! My entire body flushes with morbid embarrassment as I fidget away from him.

"Maybe," I mutter, unable to look anywhere besides my lap.

With a gentle hand, he lifts my head, forcing our eyes to meet. "It's a common thing, don't feel like you're the only one. So that's a yes?"

I nod, and very slowly he steps back, releasing his hold on my chin as well as my gaze.

"That's it then," he says, his voice reassuring. "The chemicals in the douche render the swab unreadable. We'll simply take another sample, alright?" He rolls the cart holding the tray of torture over and my spine stiffens, arms and legs nervously crossing together.

"T-take another?" I stutter.

Abruptly he turns back. "You didn't do it again today, did you?"

"No," I reply with a bit of haste and indignation. How rank does he think it is down there? *Sheesh.*

"Good. It's not recommended, ever. The vagina actually does more good for itself, naturally, if you let it. Douches strip away those good things."

"Okay." Yeah, that's all I got on the subject, not one I'm looking to discuss.

"So, alright, we'll take another pass at it. You know I have to ask, would you like—"

"Is one of your nurses begging to see my goods or what? My God, how many times must I say I'm fine without spectators?"

Scrubbing a hand over his mouth to hide the smirk, those eyes of his twinkle with amusement. "As far as I'm aware, none of my staff is vying for a peek. It's a requirement that I ask, each and every time."

I offer a grateful smile for his professionalism. "This is a small town. The less people I run into who've seen my bits, the better. No worries here. Proceed." I flop back against the table with ceremonious flair, not caring which part of my robe flies open. *Own it, right?*

Obviously taking his sweet time, I sit back up and

decide to help, attempting to go ahead and raise the stirrups for him while he does the glove/tray thing, *attempt* being the key word. I fail miserably, nearly upside down trying to pull out the difficult metal contraptions.

At the echoing clatter, his head cocks back a smidge, one brow raised. "Anxious, are we?"

I roll my eyes and sit back, realizing the stirrups are not going to cooperate. Dr. Reynolds strides over and of course makes easy work of them. *Show off.*

"Nice socks," he says with a teasing smile, guiding my feet one at time up and into place.

I shoot him a proud grin, then in one big scoot, move myself forward all the way to the end. The looming possibility of a nervous freak out is absent this time, perhaps because he's already seen all I'd kept hidden for so long.

"You remember how this works, right?" He reaches for the lamp. "Legs wide apart."

With one big breath in, I relax and allow my legs to fall open as he pulls up the bottom of my robe.

"Speculum in." He eases the cold metal inside me, then stills, waiting to hear my exhale of acceptance. "And a pinch. Good, Addison, stay relaxed for me."

It's easier this time, since I know what to expect. There's only my clammy hands and an obvious case of goosebumps, which I blame on the chill in the air, despite the heat raging under my surface. I still wonder if I feel wet, if he's using some sort of lubricant, or if the lamp is in fact the source of great heat.

"Speculum closing, and," I feel it slide from me, "out. You did great this time." He stands over me, sitting the tool on the tray. There is no quick turning around on his part, no attempt to hide the easy smile he's wearing, gentle and kind.

My breath hitches when he pulls off his gloves and tosses them in the trash beside him, never breaking the connection between us. As if I'd silently asked for more, he delicately places his hand on my calf, I assume to help lower my legs, but no. Rather, his eyes bore into my own, never wavering, as his thumb rubs slow circles over my sensitive flesh.

This I'm not imagining, or wishing—*this* is actually, tangibly happening.

I do nothing to stop him, remaining absolutely still,

focused on his powerful stare and the feel of his thumb massaging against my skin. Legs open, robe brazenly agape, I lie there unashamed, completely mesmerized.

"Addison," he murmurs in a deep timbre, "I—" His head shoots to the door.

Why sure, why wouldn't someone knock right at that exact moment? I mean, this is *my* luck we're talking about here. More disappointed than startled, I lazily sit up, drawing my legs together and straightening the robe as he moves away.

With a peek back at me, confirming that I'm composed enough to welcome a possible third party, he cracks open the door the slightest bit.

By the time he's done speaking with whomever was out in the hall and turns back, I've gotten down off the table and pulled my yoga pants up on under the robe.

"I have to go. I'll, uh, someone will call as soon as your results are in," he explains, his words unsteady.

A line has been crossed, the air surrounding us no longer heavy with intrigue and lust but awkward restlessness.

"Thank you, Doctor," I say to the floor, confusion

clouding my soft voice and dictating the downward direction of my head.

I only look up when I hear the door click. He's gone and I'm a mess of hands and feet shoving on my shirt and wrestling with my shoes. As soon as I'm fully dressed, I pull out my phone to make the call my complete bewilderment won't allow me to delay another minute.

"Jennifer, hey, it's Addison. I'll be out for the rest of the day. I'm sorry. I just finished at the doctor and I need to go home and lie down. Thank you."

DRAGGING INTO MY HOUSE, my back throbs and aches from the hunchback-ish posture that's set in with my mood. I'd fix this funk I'm in if only I knew how—usually I'm a productive, happily independent functioning member of society. Problem is, I can't pinpoint exactly what's sucked the life from me; it's just one big hodge-podge of fuzzy *ick*.

Giving no fucks that it's early afternoon, I trudge to my bedroom and slip into my comfiest pajamas, then crawl under the sanctity of my billowy down comforter. I've never been a big napper, always more important things to do in daylight, but damn if my eyelids aren't already heavy.

Everything's a wreck and I need a break from reality, so I surrender to sleep.

"Addison."

My eyes flutter open, taking in my surroundings, no longer my bedroom. Instead I'm back there, his office, sitting on the exam table wearing nothing but my lucky socks. There's no robe to cover even the smallest part of me. I'm naked, vulnerable, yet my focus is trained solely on searching for the wanting masculine voice calling out my name.

He's not in the room, not yet, but he soon will be. He's close, on the other side of that door, I can feel him. I close my eyes, imagining him standing there, ready to greet me, touch me. Is he visualizing me? Preparing his body, pleading with it to behave as I am my own?

Anticipation trembling down my legs, I watch as the door opens and he appears, calm and collected, all business. But his eyes...his eyes give him away, telling a different story. He's not just my doctor, I'm more than his patient. There's a hunger there, one that matches my own, challenging me to take what I want.

Instantly he's in front of me, as though he'd flashed across the room too quickly for the human eye to catch. No words are spoken as he lays me back, his fingers curling around my own until I'm spread out over the table.

His mouth suckles my breast, tongue flicking the nipple, hands wandering over me. He can't get enough. I can feel his excitement, his eagerness. I arch my back up, needing him closer.

He understands, walking to the end of the table and climbing up. His strong body covers my own as he claims my mouth in zealous fervor, his hard, rigid length pulsing against my stomach.

My legs creep out from under him and wrap around his back, the movement pushing his cock exactly where I need it. I feel the twitch when I grind against it.

My hands tangle in his silky hair over his shoulders, then slide between our bodies, tugging to open his pants. He places a final kiss to my collarbone then raises up to assist. My heavy lidded eyes meet Brady's familiar face suddenly looking down into mine.

"I know you want me too, Moe. Always been mine."

I throw up my hands, pushing him away, scurrying off the side of the table, now my bed, where I awaken, fingers delved in my core, body so close but mind alarmingly confused. It takes a moment to fully immerse back into consciousness.

What the hell is happening to me?

Overheated and heart pounding, I'm twisted in the

sheets, a light sheen of sweat covering my enflamed body.

My dream. Oh God, my dream.

Attempting to control my rapid breaths, I glance over at my alarm. Eight am! I'd never set it, falling asleep mid-day, and now I'm right on track to be late for work and irresponsibly unconcerned.

And like a slap in the face, my *dear* friend irony decides to pick this moment to start pounding on my front door— literally. I only have myself to blame for the early morning visitor. Finally acknowledging the silent phone on the side table, I have no doubt who it is. I climb out of bed and check that I'm presentable enough, or at least fully covered, and go answer him.

This outta be fun. *"Morning. I stopped short of what was an actual wet dream when you showed up in it. How are you today?"*

"Counting to ten, Moe, then I'm using my key!" he yells from the other side.

"Calm down, I'm coming," I mumble, swinging open the door to one frumpy-faced Brady.

"She's alive!" he snaps, showing himself in. "Here." He hands me a Starbucks cup, one quick sip confirming my favorite grande no whip peppermint white mocha.

"Is this—"

"No, after five thousand orders, I begged them to pour in an actual vat of fat. *My bad*," he deadpans. "Did you want non-fat?"

Well, someone's in a mood.

Not wanting to test the waters further, I take another sip, the harshness in his surveying eyes running the length of my front and then back up.

"Why aren't you dressed for work? And why's your phone been off since *yesterday*?"

"Morning to you too, Brady. I'm fine, thanks for asking, and my phone was switched off because as a grown ass woman. I'm allowed to do that when the mood strikes." I breeze past him in long, angry strides. *Dick!*

"Why?"

"Why what?" I huff, setting my coffee on the counter while I snatch a hair clip from the junk drawer.

"*Why* was your phone off?"

I wrap my hair in a loose bun and slide the clip in place, debating the best response, a formidable Brady looming over me. "I was tired." I turn on my heel and pry open the refrigerator in an attempt to block him out while seemingly searching for something of substance to squelch the gurgle of my empty stomach.

"Bullshit." His hand, inches from my head, slams the fridge door shut, locking me in place.

"We need to talk and you ignoring my calls and texts—" his nostrils flare, eyes hard as he leans into me, "pisses me off like nothing else."

My chin juts out in response. "That's what happens when you act like a jerk!" I shove against his chest but he doesn't budge, not even a sway.

My hands drop to my sides, pumping in and out of fists. Not because I plan to throw a punch; I've never been one to hit, but I use this to channel the rage that's about to burst from my pursed lips. And when the hell did Brady's chest get so hard?

Focus!

Unaffected, he continues as though my hands had never attacked him. "Me and you, we're gonna fight occasionally, it happens between *friends*. But you gotta answer the *fucking* phone to let a guy apologize, got it?"

"Fine. You're here now, so would you like to sit down?" I let the sarcasm drip off my words, snide smile in place over my tight lips.

"Sure, join me." He grabs my hand and pulls me into the living room and down onto the couch beside him. "Look, I'm sorry about what I said, Moe, okay? I was too…harsh."

He shakes his head, his features softening on his sigh. When he looks back up, my anger melts into hurt, reopening the wound I suffered from his callous words. But also at the regret I hold for mentioning his bastard father. I wait nervously through the silence for him to say more.

"I don't wanna fight with you, ever. You know I didn't mean a word of it. You're smart and capable and always make the best fucking decisions. I was just mad; you're kinda rough on Dylan."

I rest back against the sofa pillow, tucking one leg under me. "I seem too rough because it's always in direct comparison to you being *too* easy," I say softer, his apology already accepted. "But I agree, he needs support, so I'll be there for him. No more naysayer here."

His shoulders deflate. "Come here." He embraces me in a hug and kisses the top of my head. "Love you, Moe, so sorry. Forgive me?"

"You know I do." My head pulls back just enough to see his face. "I'm sorry I brought up your father. That was a bitch move. I didn't—"

"Stop, I'm over it. You were just angry. You and that temper of yours." A chuckle catches in his throat and I yank myself from his arms.

"I do not have a temper! I'm passionate is all!" I screech out just as Brady's arm encircles my waist and drags me down in a fighting move, pinning me underneath him.

"Passionate, huh?"

His heady scent overwhelms my frazzled senses, as does the firmness in his arms, and I'm jolted back to my dream. I can't think, can't breathe. My stomach is a swirl of butterflies and rational concerns tangled in a nasty brawl. My core's weeping, saturated with desire as his fingers dig into my hips.

"Yes, passionate, and incredibly stubborn," he murmurs, lips hovering over my ear, the weight of his chest crushing against mine.

Does he feel it too—the heat? The cruel, undeniable

link pulsing between us? Or is this just a playful match that my body is reading further into? I'm unsure, only one thought clear—get away.

With a scorching blush, I shove at him in an awkward display of gangly arms and legs, ready to start screeching, but he's already gone. He sits across from me, scrubbing his hand across his face, contemplation evident.

Keep it casual. As though I can ignore that our worlds have been totally thrown off kilter.

"Hey," I offer a silly grin, "aren't you gonna be late for work?"

"Aren't you?" His playful mood returns, lip curling up on one side with his smug retort.

"Not going in today. Gonna veg with some girly flicks, tissues, and rocky road."

Pulling me back in with an arm around my shoulder, he nuzzles his nose at my temple. It's a completely innocent and normal action, one he's done a million times, one that soothes away my apprehension. "Sounds perfect. I'm in."

So we both call in to work and for the rest of the day and reenact a scene much like the time Eric Bishop called me the night before the 9th grade formal and explained that he asked someone else before me and forgot, dumping me flat.

We wrap up in a big, comfy blanket and watch movies purposely designed to make me cry, while Brady laughs and hands me more tissues.

But this time, it's not the same Brady who joins me. I'm not sure *which* version it is—friend Brady attractive and sweet when he wants to be, or *dream* Brady. Nor am I sure how I feel about the answer…or which one I'm rooting for.

Chapter Nine

THE NEXT FIVE DAYS are perhaps the longest, most lackluster that I've ever endured. Brady's at a medical convention in California and besides a "landed safely" text, there hasn't been a word from him. Not that we usually chat a lot while he's away, but still, I notice the absence this time more than I'd like to admit.

Dylan's wrapped up in his new business, which I'm delighted by. I wouldn't dream of interrupting his newly formed work ethic, but it's another void.

And even Roscoe, the bloodhound who'd become the "Old man of the clinic," went to doggie Heaven this week.

On the afternoon of day two, it finally dawns on me—I don't have very many friends. None I'm eager to call over anyway, mostly just colleagues at the clinic. But really, aside from Brady and Dyl, I'm damn near the hermit cat lady.

I snatched up the book I'd yet to make it past the first chapter of and skimmed through a few words before realizing readings only fun if you *want* to do it, not because you're a loser with nothing else to occupy your time.

Annoyed that I had no life outside of work and the two knuckleheads, I tossed the thick paperback aside and grabbed my laptop. Scrolling through days' worth of emails, I was lead straight into the world of online shopping.

Amazing really. There is next to nothing you can't buy over the internet.

After a brief shopping spree and nearly maxing out my Amex with the gazillion dollars extra for overnight delivery, my toy box arrived in a discreet, unmarked package the next morning. Marking the "cherry popping" occasion into the ownership of "equipment," I'd gotten a variety. Red, blue, purple, innie, outie, both—you name it, I bought it.

So night three was the best I'd experienced in a while.

I learned my love lies with the blue outie flicker, and I finally got some full-fledged, definite crescendo, relief.

Day four and five consisted of nothing but work, then straight home for some Addison and "new friend" time.

Thank fuck Brady gets home tonight and I'm picking him up from the airport or I literally might cause permanent numbness to my hot spot. I could go again right now. As horny as I was before purchasing my corded companion, it's only been feeding the beast, not fully satisfying it.

All week I've done nothing but think of Dr. Reynolds; images of mussed chestnut hair, vibrant eyes, and that smile. Six feet of hard, masculine body with husky, baritone instructions, joined by an electrifying touch on constant mental reel.

While the physical release has been nirvana, it hasn't filled a deeper, emotional and mental desire. I need the weight of a man on top of me, hard and pulsing inside me as he commands my body as his own.

Once again I've lost myself in the vision of just that, head fallen back, eyes closed and panties soaked when a loud bang on the hood of my car startles me.

My head rapidly flies up, wildly blinking eyes meeting familiar green ones through the windshield.

Brady's home.

My stomach somersaults, reminding me of that whole muddled head trip I've got going on. With a confused, overwhelmed sigh, I hit the door lock then reach beneath my seat and pop the trunk. It'd of course be nicer of me to jump out and greet my oldest friend with a "welcome back" hug, but I honestly don't trust my quivering legs to hold my weight at the moment.

Just as well; he's sitting in the passenger seat smiling at me by the time I finish the thought.

"Mocifus." He leans over and engulfs me in a tight hug and lands a kiss at my temple. "Boy, did I miss you. Thanks for picking me up."

"You smell like you." *What in the name of hell, Addison? Think before you mumble, Jesus!* I'm so out of sorts these days, I simply can't be trusted to speak, ever.

He chuckles and quirks a brow, thrown off, like myself, by my crazy. "Thank you? I'm sorry? No clue on this one, babe."

Babe? Babe is new...probably residual, or actually not

even being said. First my speech, now my hearing.

In need of a buffer, I turn the key, firing up the engine and rolling out of the loading lane. Focusing on the merging vehicles such as my own, I casually toss out, "You usually come home from those conventions wreaking of the last conquest is all. Lemme guess, somebody funked up the plane's bathroom and ruined the final descent quickie this time?"

When several seconds pass without his usual witty comeback, I steal a quick glance his direction, expecting to find him dozing off.

I'm more than a bit shocked to find him silent, eyes adrift, pondering. *Come on, the flight isn't that long—surely you remember whether or not you get laid during it!*

"Actually," he mumbles, appearing dazed, "I didn't touch a single girl the entire trip. Didn't even realize. Huh," he wonders aloud.

I'd call bullshit if not for the way his brow is tugged down low, lips twitching to the side. "Wow, must've been a busy convention," I say instead.

"Not at all." Brady clears his throat and leans the seat back. He rests his head facing me with a relaxed, growing smile. "I got you something."

My head shoots his way, as does the wheel, and his hand flies up to correct it. I smack it away, my full attention back on the road.

"Shit!" I sputter under my breath, ignoring the blare of the horn from the car beside me that I damn near sideswiped.

He bought me a something? On one of his trips? That's a first.

"Damn, Moe, you okay?"

Eyes straight, I weave into the turning lane and finally merge onto the interstate. "Yeah, sorry. So, uh, let me get this straight, you didn't get laid all week, but you bought your best friend's little sister a gift? You feeling okay over there?"

He chuckles. "Never been better. I was just at the beach there and—"

"Shut up! No way *you* went to the beach and didn't take at least one surf bunny back to the hotel." I laugh.

Brady's always been into sports and with that comes the flocks of swooning girls, especially when he's at the beach. Not gonna lie, I've gawked at him on his board a few times myself over the years. It's purely human nature, appreciating a beautiful creature out in the elements—it can't be helped.

"I stayed on land this time." He digs around in his pocket. "Here."

I glance over and see the tiny wooden surfboard attached to a key chain. "Addison engraved down the front surprises me, he rarely uses my real name.

He places it in my hand and my heart can't help but swell.

"Thank you." The air shifts, his scrutiny set my way. "So did you grab it in the airport gift shop? My name's getting easier to find on those racks." I chuckle in a vain attempt to deflect the becoming familiar but still undefined intensity. I quickly remind myself it doesn't mean anything; he's bought me birthday and Christmas gifts before, no difference.

"No, Moe, I had it engraved for you."

I swallow. "Oh, well…um, I love it. Maybe one day you'll get me on a real board." I peek his way to find he's still staring, a thoughtful smile in place.

"One day."

Silence. That's all there is for two and a half long drawn out minutes. Seriously, I'm watching the clock. I've never sat up so straight in my life, unsure of myself but intensely aware of every move he makes. His left hand slips down his thigh, resting on his knee. Fingers tap in an uneven beat. His other hand tucks under his head in a makeshift pillow. Then there's his breathing that occasionally releases a slight "hmm."

I hear it all, feel it all, and it leaves me with nothing but scattered thoughts and a tight grip on the steering wheel.

"So what'd you do while I was gone?"

I flinch at his words slicing through the silence. DO. NOT. JUST. ANSWER. ADDISON. STOP. DROP. AND THINK BEFORE TALKING.

"Read some," I reply quickly. "Laundry."

"Rebel," he mocks me with a snort. "How's Dyl?"

"Good question. I haven't heard a peep. I'm hoping he's swamped with a flourishing new business." I peek over my shoulder, making sure I'm clear to switch lanes. "Why don't you call him real quick, see if he's up for dinner. My treat. Unless you're too tired?"

"Dillweed," his boom cuts me off, already on the

phone. Not too tired. "You work too hard brother. Awesome. Yeah can't wait to see. Hey, so Moe and I are picking you up in thirty for dinner. *My treat.*"

―――――

THE NEXT MORNING I'm slow to rise and spend most of it in my pajamas, puttering around. God bless Saturdays. I re-do my nails a cheerful bright pink, wash sheets, and water all my plants, feeling caught up and accomplished. Then, I tackle the dreaded mail pile. It's a "quirk" about me, one that Brady and Dylan both love to ridicule. I refuse to conform to online billing and automatic drafts. They take money out of your account? Bullshit! Yes, I realize it's on a set date, but who remembers all of them, every month? Not me. Nor do I want the agony of opening a new bill each day, so my system is stack all week, open everything all at once on the weekend.

Brilliant, I say.

Halfway through the pile, my plan's failing already, dismay settling in by the fifth invoice, when the bottom of my stomach drops, as well as my jaw.

There's an envelope from Dr. Reynolds' office. My

test results.

Even though he assured me it was most likely the douche that caused the initial inconclusive results, there's still a chance of something else, something serious. My heart's racing, a throb building in my temple as unsteady hands struggle to open the letter.

Blowing out a joyful squeal, my eyes read down the column of one "normal" after another. I leap to my feet, tossing the letter in the air as I jubilantly bust out a happy dance.

Shaking my ass, arms above my head, I send up a silent "thank you" to Heaven followed by an air blown kiss. After a few more ridiculous moves, my body begins to slow, breathing heavily, but happily.

I'm okay.

And then...I'm so much more than okay. When I bend down to pick up the strewn papers from the floor, a small Post-it falls out.

In masculine, but surprisingly legible handwriting, the words jump off the page and tug ruthlessly at the depths of me.

Addison,

Had these rushed. No more worries, you're perfect.

Dr. R

I'm pretty level headed, except lately, and somewhat of a realist, so I've already second guessed the double-entendres of the phrases he's used, the heavy breaths I thought I heard and every other "little something" my mind's been telling me was there. Yes, I'm young and admittedly not well-seasoned on matters of the heart or to gyno visits and what they normally entail. But I am positive—heart fluttering, full-body tingles, panties sweating positive that the note currently crushed to my chest is special.

Too anxious to worry or even recall the fact that it's Saturday, I grab my phone, fingers itching to dial, unsure yet of my guise or master plan... I just have to act, have to jump and see where I fall.

Divinely, someone picks up on the second ring. "Dr. Reynolds' answering service."

Crap. I chomp down on my bottom lip. "Oh, yes hello. Um, so the office isn't open today?"

"No ma'am, but we can help you. Is this an

emergency?"

"N-no, not an emergency," I stammer, contemplating if my racing pulse can be declared an emergency.

"Are you an expectant mother or in labor?"

"No, I—" My words fall off. *Think!* What do I want? "I need to make an appointment," I recite calmly. There we go—agenda set on its own.

She proceeds to ask me a series of way too intrusive questions to ascertain if my appointment can indeed wait and be scheduled at a later date. I pass her test, insisting I need to get on the books as soon as possible. In her monotone rambling, she recites several days and times as choices, and I immediately cut in and choose the soonest— Monday at four.

Excellent.

Only two days away and merely an hour of work missed. The rest of the weekend, said no one, ever, drags by.

Chapter Ten

FEELING GOOD, fresh as a daisy and sexy as ever, I'm perched on the edge of the exam table, fully dressed and impossibly anxious, swinging my crossed ankles back and forth in anticipation. I'd opted not to don the robe, mildly confident that the brilliant excuse I've concocted doesn't call for it, but took care of all my pre-game prep, minus the douche, *in case it does.*

Unlike before, when he knocks lightly and sticks his head in today, I'm not trying to make myself as small as possible with my head down. Rather, my chin and chest are up and proud, my eyes meeting his dead-on.

"Hi, Dr. Reynolds," I greet him first.

"Addison," he draws out my name in a low, tantalizing hum and steps fully inside, shutting the door behind him. "To what do I owe the pleasure?"

My guess would be that smile, voice, body and sexual prowess. But just a guess.

"The appointment sheet says you called over the weekend. Everything alright? Did you get your results? They were mailed the other day, all normal." Eyes taking on concern, he steps closer.

"I got them, yes and I saw, *perfect*. Thank you." I suck in my bottom lip, allowing the words to linger and speak for themselves.

With a hint of a blush, his unease disappears, replaced with a playful sparkle in his dazzling eyes. "You got my note then?"

Still chewing my bottom lip flirtatiously, I answer with a nod.

No mistaking it, he releases a low hiss, his eyes skating over me once. I uncross my legs and place my hands on each side of myself on the table, waiting for him to take the lead.

He clears his throat and steps back as if escaping a trance. "What can I help you with today?"

"I'd like to start some birth control."

I'd googled "top reasons women go to the gyno" and this was the least unpleasant topic *and* can't be disproven. Plus, if things in reality ever catch up to my dreams, I'll need it. The ideal ploy.

"Oh?" Both his dark brows shoot to his matching hairline. "That was fast. You just adamantly declined needing it not too damn long ago."

Did he just cuss?

He takes a seat on his stool. "What's changed?"

I laugh and give him a questioning smirk of my own. You'd think the doctor in the room would understand precisely what *change* would make a woman suddenly need birth control, but I realize the hilarity could backfire and my laughter's cut short. I don't want him to think I'm unavailable. Shit! Curse fake plans and their unforeseen potholes.

"Nothing, yet. I just figured..." I shrug, glancing around the room with nonchalance. "Since I'm taking care of everything else, might as well be prepared there too."

He remains silent, regarding me with curious eyes a few moments before finally consulting the chart. "Did you have a particular method in mind?"

"Nope. Can you tell me the options?"

"The most common of course, is a daily birth control pill. Women your age, nonsmokers, have good results with it, and it's the most affordable up front."

"What if you forget to take it?" I question. "And don't a lot of women gain weight from it?"

He nods, setting down the chart and making eye contact, apparently ready to have a natural conversation. "Those are both concerns I hear quite often. Another option is the Depo shot. It lasts for three months at a time, so you don't have to worry about forgetting anything." He grins. "Except scheduling the next shot. I will warn you though, a lot of recipients experience months of bleeding initially, then none at all. And weight gain's a common complaint with this one as well."

"They should hire you for PR," I jest. "Lemme think." I tap my chin. "A pill I'll probably forget or a needle, with month-long periods and extra weight. Hmmm, tempting, but I'll pass, on both."

He chuckles and nods. "Okay, what about an IUD?"

"Which is?"

"Intrauterine Device. Let me show you one." He stands and opens the door, asking a nurse to bring him a Mirena demo.

Meanwhile, I'm breaking down word parts to figure out what we're talking about here.

Intra-in.

Uterine-my uterus.

Device-technical, scary word, especially when preceded by IN.MY.UTERUS.

My mouth's open, fully prepared to bark "next," when he shuts the door and sits down in front of me again.

"This is an IUD." He holds up a small piece of T-shaped plastic. "It's inserted into your uterus and you use the small threads to check its placement once a month. After inserted, neither you nor your partner should be able to feel it." He gently takes my hand and places the device in my palm so I can familiarize myself.

"It can last as long as five years, or five days, you choose. The effective rate is over 99% and is completely reversible at any time."

I eye the tiny possibility I'm holding. "Does it hurt?"

"When it goes in, you'll feel a brief pinch and there may be mild cramps or even bleeding for a few days after, but then you should be fine. Also, it's unlikely, but if you were to become pregnant with the IUD in place, it will almost definitely cause an ectopic pregnancy."

My head snaps up at that and a frown curves his lips at my bleak expression. *Is there no flawless birth control out there?*

"Sorry, just want you to have all the facts."

"I understand." Someday I'd love children but I'm not there yet. "Anything else?" I ask.

"Yes, and this is very important." He rolls an inch closer, expression turning deadly serious. "An IUD isn't recommended for women who aren't monogamous. Are you planning on a relationship...*is he*?"

"Wh—" I squeak, abhorred. I shove my body back, spine pin straight. "Can you ask that? He who? You...ugh," I growl, flustered to the point of incoherency.

"Addison," his voice is low and sinister as he places a firm hand on my knee and squeezes, "an IUD leaves you *highly* susceptible to infection. I can't advise it in good faith and I'll refuse to insert it unless you can assure me you fully understand the risk."

How has this appointment taken such an ugly, drastic turn? I wanted to see him, and my *safe* excuse plan is backfiring like a rusty old truck. Did I not already tell him this was precautionary? There is no *he*, yet... and I'd wasted my time coming today since Dr. Reynolds is obviously under the assumption I'm ready to "cat around" with...someone who's not him.

My embarrassment at how grossly I'd misread things, conjuring up this apparently non-existent, cockamamie connection that's left me the fool, quickly morphs to anger.

"Never mind." I shake my head, fighting back threatening, humiliated tears. I attempt to scramble down from the table as quickly and gracefully as possible. "I-I was just researching," I mumble.

"Addison." The hand on my arm, as stern as his gravelly voice, stalls my hasty, teary retreat.

"I'm fine. This was...I just...thought I'd play it safe but..." I blow out a sigh, ending my rambles.

"Sit back down, please." His tone is soft, sweet, coercing; I settle again on the table, eyes downcast. "Take a breath."

Long, silent moments pass and I remain stoic in my tight-lipped avoidance, so he gently lifts my chin, forcing to me to look at him. "If you want the IUD, and can promise me that you'll ask any guy you date to be tested before intercourse...then I'll put it in." His hand falls away. "I'm sorry if I upset you. That wasn't my intention, I just...want you safe is all."

"Thank you," I say in a whisper. Rebuilding my confidence, I look him in the eyes and ask, "Can you put it in today?"

"Yes."

"Okay, I want the IUD...today...and I promise I'll be safe."

He says nothing, only offers a slow nod of understanding. "Go ahead and undress." He pulls a robe from a drawer and hands it to me. "I'll be back in a couple minutes."

"Okay," I echo my previous response.

He searches my eyes, where I'm sure he finds curiosity mixed with a hint of excitement, but no anxiety or fear. His lip quirks slightly before he seemingly comes to terms with my decision and turns to leave the room.

I undress and pull on the robe like the pro I'm becoming. By the time I'm back in place on the table, his knock sounds.

"Come in," I call out and watch as the door opens and he steps in holding a tray.

I lie back and he rolls the stool to the end of the table and guides my feet into the stirrups. At this point it's routine, no spoken directions, our movements syncing rhythmically.

"You ready?" he asks.

I tuck my arms behind my head to help prop me up a bit. "Yeah."

There's the familiar coolness of the speculum, his fingers spreading me as he slides it in. "Alright, here we go. You're gonna feel a little stick when I place the IUD and that's it."

The *stick* is more like a shot to a place you really don't want one. I suck in a deep hiss through gritted teeth at the stab, my entire body clenching. It's quick though, and before I even completely open my tightly closed eyes, I feel the speculum sliding out.

"All done." I hear the tool clank down on the tray

followed by the pop of his gloves as he pulls them off. "You okay?"

I catch my breath. "It felt like a bee flew in there and stung me."

He chuckles softly, still on his stool between my open legs. "Sorry. Wish there was something I could do."

"Do you?" That just came out but I don't wish it back. I leave it out there for him to decipher, which he does.

Highly attuned to the shift in the air, I feel a soft brush along my inner thigh, seconds before a warm stream of breath tickles my flesh, directed at my center. His breath? I peer down at him over my stomach but all I see is his hair. It's unmistakable though. He's blowing on me soothingly and then...I suck in a deep inhale when I feel his hands on my inner thighs, *so close* to where I ache for him.

Are we really doing this?

"Addison..." he rumbles, voice unsteady.

"Yes." I arch upward, answering both of our unspoken questions, giving him permission.

His hand cups my sex, taking what he wants, his breathing staggered and echoing around us.

I wiggle in a pleading move and his hand brushes

down over me, slowly parting my damp center. His finger caresses, flicking over my clit.

"Please," I moan.

That's all it takes to compel him further, a thick, strong finger slipping inside me, stroking with deliberate but gentle motions. His other hand grips my thigh, as though for support, as his thrusting grows faster, more urgent. I counter, slamming myself downward, riding now two fingers shamelessly, shocked but delighted that I feel no pain, only ecstasy.

It feels torturously right, everything I'd been craving, or so I thought… until his rough tongue wisps over my clit and I cry out, knowing "everything" just got so much better. That's all it takes for me to come undone right there on the exam table and I'm lost, conscious of nothing but the wave of tingling bliss rolling its way through my entire body.

He slows his ministrations, lapping gently as I ease back down to Earth, then slides his fingers out as he rises to stand, towering over me. He holds me captive in his stare, chin and mouth still glistening of "me," as unsure of what to say as I am. My ogle wanders over his broad chest to pants, drawn tight, perfectly outlining his massive erection. I sit up, ready to relieve him when he steps back and turns around.

"T-that shouldn't have happened," he stammers. "I'm sorry. I've never…with a patient… I-I've never—"

"I wanted you to. Blame me."

He turns back to face me just as another knock interrupts us. I'm probably his longest appointment ever. I can only imagine what the other patients or worse, the nurses, think.

"I have to go," he says, walking to the door.

"Of course."

He gives a curt nod and opens the door when I say in a whisper, "Thank you."

Chapter Eleven

As though drifting on a cloud, I float mindlessly around the gym the next morning, afterglow still on megawatt.

Say goodbye to my little blue friend.

So much better when delivered by the firm, capable hands of a sexy, titillating man.

It may have ended somewhat uncomfortably, but the beautiful damage was already done, the effects still a tingling reminder between my legs.

Just thinking back to it, his deep, heavy breaths, my legs wide and seductive as he strummed my body like his favorite instrument, has me wet and wanting to make a whole damn album.

"What's got you smiling?"

I jolt as Brady sneaks up behind me and husks in my ear, blushing wildly, afraid he can read my mind. "H-hey," I sputter, shaking off residual ecstasy. I tilt my head to him. "Nothing really, just in a good mood."

"Mhmm," he hums, leaning in closer to run his nose up to my neck. "Fuck, you smell like sin, Moe."

It's probably the pheromones. Every dog in the clinic will like me today.

While I'm caught in drifting thoughts, he's somehow managed to entwine our hands and sequester me in the men's locker room.

Oh no. I know what he does in here! I'm not *that* horny!

"Brady," I look around, shocked that he's dragged me in here so quickly, "What the—how'd—what are we doing in here?"

He laughs and taps my nose. "Not that, unless of course, you beg." His playful simper edged with seriousness. "Kidding. I just wanted to talk to you, privately."

"Okay," I hedge.

"There's something here," he croons.

"What? Where?" Hyperaware of the dank locker room, I warily look around again.

"No, not in this room. You know what I'm talking about, Moe."

"I do?" I reply in a passive drivel.

"Don't play coy with me. Things are different between us. We're not the same friends we used to be. It's all I can think about." He steps into me and moves a piece of hair behind my ear.

Why, oh why, does he have to go there? No way I'm answering him and especially not agreeing, instead eyeing him suspiciously as the crickets chirp. But he waits for me to shatter the calm.

"Brady," I mutter, voice shaky, eyes cast at the ground. "We can't."

"Can't what?" He bends and ducks his head below mine, forcing me to look at him. "So you do know what I'm talking about. Which must mean you feel it too?"

"Women in Antarctica can feel it," I deflect in cowardice. "You're single, gorgeous, successful, brilliant..." My words die off softly.

"So half as amazing as you then." He slides a finger under my chin and guides my dropped head up. "Only care what you're feeling, Moe."

Brady... my friend, truly the best one I have. My rock, my always and unfailing, my dependable. *No way am I risking that.*

My head must be shaking with the protest I'm devising because his hand shoots out and slams against the locker he's backed me up to, startling me.

"Bullshit. Don't deny it. Something's changed between us and I want it. So do you! I can see the pulse in your neck." He dips to my ear, releasing a deep, carnal growl. "I can smell it."

"Wh-what?" I gasp.

"Mm huh, you're thinking of all the bad in that head of yours, but your body's telling mine yes, loud and clear." He pulls me into his arms and places a kiss above my ear." Let's try, Moe."

My eyes close, heightening my other senses. I can smell him too—Brady on fire. I stand there in his arms and lazily stroke my hands up and down his back, absorbing the closeness. That is, until his growing erection digs against my stomach and his struggle to tame his breathing douses me with a cold gush of reality.

My hands still halfway down his spine and I step out of his hold. "Brady," I groan in regret, "you're one of the most important people in the world to me. I love you and couldn't live without you. And that's why..." I sigh, blinking back tears. "That's why I need you to walk away, right now."

After what feels like forever, a mixed current of temptation and hesitance buzzing between us, he turns with a hard set to his features and storms from the room, leaving me crushed and despondent. I hear him mumble "coward" on his way out, breaking another piece of my heart.

<hr />

THE NEXT FEW days crawl by, no, scratch that, they drag like a dyslexic fucking slug. Obviously I haven't talked to Brady, my brother's once again buried in "Game On!"—I love the name—my parents flew themselves to Bermuda, and I'll be damned if I can think of a halfway viable excuse to go see Dr. Reynolds.

So at this point, I owe it to society to wear a t-shirt

that says "Turn around, cross the street or call 9-1-1, you've been warned."

And in a cruel joke by the gods of irony, it's Thursday, Tiko night. Imagine that. Either I ditch, looking even more the coward, or I go, stupidly hoping the tension will be less than that of chewing glass.

Decisions, decisions.

I've got the quarter in my hand, ready to flip my destiny, when it dawns on me. The very reason I shunned Brady's advances was for the sake of our friendship, the very one I'm debating bailing on tonight.

Coward *and* a hypocrite? Not this girl! With new determination, I drag myself down the hall and prepare for Tiko night with an optimistic attitude and maybe a lil extra attention to my appearance.

I'm the first to arrive, visiting with Juan when Dylan comes busting in, looking frazzled.

"Well, hello, stranger." I lean forward to give him a kiss on the cheek. "How are you?"

"Wiped." He turns to Juan and slaps him on the shoulder. "Make 'em extra strong tonight, my man."

With a chuckle, Juan hurries away to get our pitcher of

margaritas as Dylan takes a seat.

"Where's Brady?"

Tapering my expression, I answer as naturally as possible. "I'm not sure, apparently running l—"

Or running game! My voice catches as Brady and date walk in hand in hand.

"Don't screw with sanctity of our night, not cool," my ass!

"'Only care what you're feeling, Moe,'" my butt!

"Hey guys, sorry we're late. Ashley had to take an important work call outside," Brady greets us, pulling out the chair beside me for her. "Dylan, Addison, this is Ashley Chastain. She's the Assistant Administrator at the hospital." He helps her into a chair with a gentle hand to her back, avoiding my glare, then takes the chair across from me.

"It's nice to meet you both," she says with a smile. "Brady told me a bit about you on the way over." Her smile is warm, genuine, and when combined with her huge brown eyes, olive complexion and long raven hair…it makes for one remarkable package.

I flag my hand in the air, desperate for a drink.

Unable to keep from peeking over at her, the rare "brains and beauty exotic princess," who has six inches on me—height and bust—I rape the pitcher from Juan's hands when he divinely appears at my side. Hand shaking as I pour, I'm hoping the penis-packers are too mesmerized by Ashley to notice.

The woman's breathtaking.

"Nice to meet you too," I finally manage to get in between Dylan's long winded introduction that includes way too much info about his day spent scouting employees.

"So you and Brady know each other from the hospital then, I assume?" Dylan asks, ceasing the recital of his recent new bio as I get a head start on my life-or-death buzz.

"Yes." She reaches across and lays her hand atop Brady's, caressing his knuckles with her pristinely manicured thumb. "We see each other there often. I couldn't believe he finally asked me out." She turns her head and gives him a sultry smile.

"When was that?" I ask a bit too enthusiastically, already knowing the answer *and* that Brady's sneer is pinned on me right this minute.

"Oh, well today's Thursday, so I guess it was…Tuesday? Is that right?" she asks him.

Huh, how very interesting! I slurp down another mouthful of margarita. Tuesday, the same day as our anything-but-amicable parting at the gym...you don't say.

"Sounds right, gorgeous." He lifts her hand to his mouth and places a kiss on the back of it. "The morning you gave the proposal on the new NICU unit you brilliantly assembled."

"That's cool," Dylan cuts in animatedly. "I'm leading a new project myself, a gaming software company that Brady here is backing. Thus the need for employees, which has kept me tied up all week. Brady's gonna help me look over resumes this weekend, right?" He nudges Brady in the shoulder with a grin.

"Appears so," Brady replies, always willing to help Dylan.

"That's wonderful," Ashley says with a kind smile then turns those sincere eyes on me. "And what do you do, Addison?"

Swallowing down my huge, unladylike sip, I hold up a finger, refusing to wince at the brain freeze. Gonna need a second. Once it's down I find my voice. "I work at a veterinary clinic."

"That's wonderful. I've always admired how much schooling veterinarians have to endure. Good for you!"

I'd slap the grin off her face if it wasn't...nice. She's not usual Brady Bimbo. She's glamorous, well-educated and versed, elegant and kind. Dammit, where's Juan with a new pitcher?

"Oh, Moe's not a veterinarian, she's a vet tech," Dylan, the flesh of my flesh, lovingly corrects her.

"Only because she chooses to be." For the first time all night Brady finds and holds my gaze. "Moe can be anything she wants. But only she knows what that is. The rest of us might *think* we understood what she wanted, but we'd be wrong. Isn't that right, Addison?"

He thinks he's so clever, that I don't see through his games, defending me because it's ingrained in him to do so, ruining it with the reminder dig at the end.

And the date? I can't decide if he brought her because she's her—an admittedly smart choice—or to make me jealous—also a smart choice. If the latter, it worked like a charm, although I have no right to be jealous. *I* refused *him*.

My mood was shitty before all this fun. I don't need extra help picking the bridge to plummet from.

I'm out.

I stand and grab my purse, squaring my shoulders and chin before speaking. "I don't have some big excuse concocted for leaving. I just am." I look down at the date that fits in better at the table than I do. "Nice to meet you, Ashley."

It'd be nice to pull off an exit half as graceful as her entrance, because I can feel all their eyes upon me, but I don't stand a chance. So instead, in an average pace, I escape through the door to my clunker car, all the way to my mediocre apartment.

Not bothering to get undressed, I kick off my shoes, wash my face, scrub my teeth then hole up under the covers. I don't dream of Brady or Dr. Reynolds, but rather a time when I felt nothing new for either of them.

Chapter Twelve

THE MINUTE I'm done with work on Friday, I drive straight to my parent's house, bags already in the car. With them gone on yet another vacation, I plan to enjoy the bigger house alone. Yes, I'm hiding from it all, even if just for a weekend.

I need to get back in touch with the old Addison, the version of myself who knew what she wanted and went after it. The girl who always felt good enough in her own skin, didn't fight with her friends all the time, and was content even when by herself.

I park in the less noticeable car port on the side and

head in with only my purse and duffle—no phone. Luckily, their alarm code is still mine and Dyl's birthdays, so I get past that easily and go straight to turn on the hot tub and heater on the pool—just in case.

Oh nice, they finally had the pool resurfaced, the bottom no longer sporting "Bad Bros 4 Life" with a poorly drawn skull and crossbones in black spray paint at the bottom. To this day, Dyl and Brady swear they weren't under the influence of any illegal substances and simply thought it seemed like a really cool idea at the time. My parents did not agree.

Snickering at the memory, I head to the kitchen, craving a glass of wine…and am assaulted with yet another memory. There, on the fridge, is a picture of the three of us—the little girl with the bowl haircut standing between her two older, much taller heroes—all smiling at the camera.

As I trace my fingertip over it, I notice that which I never have before; Brady's not looking at the camera, but rather, eyes angled down at me.

Even when I come here, searching an escape, it's not in the cards…Brady is so deeply rooted in my life, wherever I am, a part of him will be there as well.

And this is pretty much how I spend my entire weekend. Reminders lurk around every corner, triggering fond flashbacks that make our current, floundering friendship even more painful. No matter how many hot soaks I take, the two bottles of wine mysteriously becoming three, or the 400 page hot ménage m/f/m romance novel I use to fill the hours, most of the weekend is spent reminiscing about times when Brady and I knew exactly what "Brady and I" meant.

All too soon, it's time to pull up my big girl panties and head back to reality. Putting clean sheets on the bed and a "thank you for your unknown hospitality, love you both" note on the counter, I grumble all the way to my car.

I have to snicker at myself as I settle into the driver's seat. What the hell did we all do before cell phones? It's the first thing I check, ending my bout of abstinence.

There's three texts from Brady.

One on Friday night. **Nothing happened w/ Ashley. Call me.**

Another Saturday afternoon. **Where the fuck are u?! Worried!**

And the last one a few hours ago. **You break my heart.**

I refused a "go" with Brady to protect our friendship, and it appears it's had the opposite effect.

———————⟨⟩———————

I KINDA already know I look like the walking dead after not a wink of sleep last night, but when Mimi won't come near me when I open the clinic Monday morning, I really feel disgusting.

Making the rounds of morning feedings, I add an extra coo to my voice to hopefully offset my haggard appearance, but it only works on the animals under any sort of sedation, the rest not buying my act.

At lunch I sit and eat in my car, barely choking down a banana and Gatorade. I'm feeling so leprous that I actually squeal when my phone rings, amazed someone's calling me.

"Hello?"

"Miss Porter?"

"Yes."

"This is Dr. Reynolds' office. He'd like you to come in for a follow up from your last appointment. What day is good for you?"

Follow up? Last visit I came, hard, the end. But if he wants to follow that up…

"Whatever day you have, but afternoon. I'd like to try to miss as little work as possible."

"Understandable. Let me see…he has 4:30 today, 3:30 on Wednesday, or 4:30 on Friday."

Not quite as anxious this time, but equipped with almost no patience, I confirm for today's slot. Ending my lunch early, I go back inside to make sure Whitney or Jennifer are okay covering the last part of the afternoon for me, which they generously agree to with comforting hugs.

～

AT 4:37, I find myself sitting on the exam table, nervously awaiting what's to be between the Dr. and I this time.

The door opens as he knocks, his face solemn but still gorgeous. "Addison," he acknowledges me stiffly. "How are you? Nice weekend?"

I shrug, squirming under his icy regard. "Not bad, relaxing. You?"

"Quite the opposite, actually." He doesn't sit on his stool, instead standing before me, his feet spread wide and arms crossed over his chest. Hope I'm the only one who noticed he didn't bring in my chart.

"Addison, I spent my entire weekend thinking about you, and the whole week before it as well." He inhales deeply. "I've never touched a patient unprofessionally, but when I'm touching you—" He puffs his cheeks and blows out in a loud bout of contemplation then lowers his voice an octave. "When I'm touching you, you're not a patient, only Addison Porter. I brought you in today to talk, to see where you're at with everything."

Quite honestly, I'm in the midst of déjà vu.

"I like you, Addison. My attraction is almost painful and I'm drawn to you in a million other ways I can't even describe. I was hoping you'd come to the same conclusions I have." He steps closer and takes my hand. "Have dinner with me?"

Men do the detached, "when it works for me" thing all the time! I start one scandalous, liberating rendezvous and I'm pinned from all sides like a butterfly to a board.

No, no, no. I've been brazen and mysteriously enthralled for less than a month and I'm not giving it up yet!

"I like things the way they are. In this room, so many possibilities, private sessions where we test the boundaries...our sexual sanctuary," I snicker, biting my bottom lip, tempting him.

It doesn't seem to work. His brows knit together and he shifts back, pained. "Addison, in this room, you're my patient. And I can't touch a patient the way I want to touch you...the way I did the last time." His head drops as he shoves his hands deep in his pockets with a frustrated sigh. The gesture stretches the fabric of his slacks, making it clear how hard he's fighting this.

I slink off the table and move up against his front, wrapping my arms around his waist and peering up at him from under my lashes. "Then I'll touch you," I murmur in a seductive purr, licking my lips. This may be crazy but my brazen lust can't be contained.

"Addi—"

"Shhh," I lay a finger to his lips, delicately quieting him, "let me take care of the doctor." I let both my hands slide gradually down his torso, savoring the feel of carved muscles until I reach his waist.

Our eyes hold each other's captive, my own yearning

desire reflected back at me, each wanton craving matched. I undo his belt, grinning at him as I unbutton and tease open his zipper, stealing a quick glance down to gauge exactly what awaits me.

With one fingertip, I glide from the bottom all the way up his rock-hard length with provocative fluidity, ending at the weeping, engorged head peeking beyond the waistline of his black boxer briefs.

"Very nice," I praise. "I knew it would be."

One low, menacing growl and he grabs around the back of my neck, pulling my mouth to his own. His kiss is ravenous, animalistic and demanding, shoving his tongue past my parted lips and flicking against mine. The domineering kiss is effortless to follow, so I reach between us and shove down his briefs, releasing his pulsating cock.

His moan is absorbed into our kiss when I wrap my hand around as much of his velvet girth as I can manage.

With a squeeze, I stroke down to the base. He grunts, releasing my mouth and resting his forehead to mine while one of his own hands reaches around and grips my ass, squeezing almost painfully.

My heart races, pounds as quickly as my hand does,

jacking up and down his length. I can't wait another second. With some struggle, I break from his hold and drop gracefully to my knees on the cold, hard floor. I don't care though, too hungry to have the huge, pulsing dick in front of me in my mouth. Wetting my lips, slowly relishing the sight, I take as much of him in as I can in a single motion, inhaling the virile, exotic scent from the few, fine hairs tickling my nose.

He's all man; it seeps from his pores and overwhelms my senses.

"Fuck, Addison," he hisses, tangling his long, talented fingers in my hair. "So good." His whole body shudders as I swirl my tongue along his length, then underneath the ridge of the head. I cup his balls with lustful aggression, squeezing and rolling, and I swear his knees start to rock, about to buckle.

Hell yes. I'm undoing him, showing him exactly the carnal heat I want in this room. Over and over, I coat him, sucking his whole length to the back of my throat then pleasing his hole with the tip of my tongue.

"Such a good girl," he moans, kneading the back of my head. "Goddamn, Addison, suck it, babe, suck my cock."

He's unraveling; deep pants, sighs, grunts and pulsing against my tongue spur me on, craving his surrender. I'm heady with power, wet from it myself.

"Gonna cum, baby, take it for me."

I peer up at him, his penetrating stare already upon me.

"You want it all, don't you?"

Without breaking stride or suction, I grip down harder on his tightening sac and press my tongue as hard as I can against the bulging vein running down his cock. I know I have him when he holds my head forcefully still and surges his hips forward, thrusting in maddening jerks.

"Fuck yes! Ah, Addison, love your fucking mouth, baby," he garbles, flooding my mouth with his warm, salty load.

I drag off him leisurely, sucking off every last drop, then sit back on my heels while he recovers. He fixes his pants and belt, his softened, relaxed expression focused on my face as he does so, then he bends and scoops me up to stand nuzzled against his chest.

"One date," he whispers against my forehead.

I shake my head and stretch back, offering a flirty twist of my swollen lips to soften the blow. "Only here." I press my lips to his once, stepping back before he can pull me in for more. "Your secretary knows where to find me."

Fully aware he's watching, I sashay with as much saucy sex appeal as I possess out the door.

Chapter Thirteen

"MISS PORTER?"

"Yes?" I try desperately to hide the snicker in my reply. Honestly, what must they be thinking? I go from never gracing their office in my life to racking up frequent fellatio miles in a blink. Since the appointment where I dropped to my knees, I've been back twice more in the last week.

The good doctor seems to love the taste of my pussy just as much as I love the feel of his fingers inside me and the throb of his smooth, hard dick on my tongue.

"I'm sorry," *don't be,* "but Dr. Reynolds needs you to come in again as soon as possible. Is there any way you're free this afternoon?"

Acting inconvenienced, which I've almost mastered, I

sigh in her ear. "I suppose I can use my lunch break, if that'll work?"

"Wonderful. I'll make room. We'll see you then."

I hang up with a smug smile dancing over my lips, knowing I'm ready for him. Almost habit, I now take special care getting ready for work each morning, the mystery of when a call might come an exhilarating game I love to play.

The office visits are unlike anything I've ever experienced, sublime in every way except one—I haven't felt that hard shaft of his inside me where I want it most. There's never enough time, or so he uses as his excuse, anyway. Always foreplay, ending in mind-blowing orgasms, followed by his request for a real date, which I continue to reject, and then he's out the door.

Surprisingly, this game of cat and mouse keeps me so occupied that it's only spare, passing moments, such as now, that I miss Brady and Dylan, our familiar camaraderie still all but vanished. The three of us haven't hung out in ages, mostly because of Dylan's new job, but when he cancelled on the past Tiko night, Brady and I both easily accepted, not wanting to see each other, I suppose.

That's not entirely true; I'd like to spend time with Brady, but only if it's like before. All I can do is chuckle facetiously at the repeating ironic thought—protecting the friendship has vanquished it.

Luckily, I'm forced to abandon such melancholy thoughts and plaster on a smile for the rambunctious Jack Russell and its frazzled owner that walk through the door of the clinic. After checking them in, I show them back to a room and take basic preliminary information before stepping out, a glance at the clock on the wall confirming it's time to head out for lunch.

Driving to my "appointment," my tummy's a tingle, nervous anticipation coursing through my limbs as I conjure up what scenarios might play out today.

Growing more daring with each visit, I'm currently dressed in baggy scrubs. Under them is a pleated light pink skirt that stops just below my ass cheeks and a short white halter top. The second the nurse shuts the door, I'll shed the deceptive outer layer and wait impatiently, dressed like the minx I feel.

Fifteen minutes later and I'm doing exactly that, wetting my lips and pulling the band out of my hair, letting my soft mane fan out, then daintily crossing my legs. Dr. Reynolds walks in, sans knock, his eyes immediately aflame as he takes me in. His tongue darts out, creeping along a full bottom lip as he shoves a chair up under the door knob—much sexier in my dreams, when there's a lock.

"You look…" he drops his gawk from me to the floor, followed by a subtle shake of his head. Regrouping perhaps, he raises his attention back up and inches closer, his face tight. "I wanted you to join me for lunch," he declares. His voice is strong, final, his eyes on mine despite my attempt to offer up my breasts in coercion.

"Here I am," I purr, snaring him by the belt loops, pulling him between my legs.

"I see that." It's a low growl as his predatory regard finally runs the length of me again. "But I want an *actual* lunch." He gestures his head to the side and it's only now that I notice a plastic bag, obviously holding take-out, on the counter. Funny how it completely escaped my wanton attention, smell and all.

"You won't go out for a meal with me, so I brought it in. Thought we could make some semblance of dating conversation over a meal."

Seriously, years of nothing and I finally release my inner sex kitten only to be brow-beaten with courtship? Women would kill to be in my shoes, and all I want is to be out of them... and my panties.

"Don't." I loosen his necktie, moving straight to the buttons of his dress shirt. "Things are perfect the way they are. Can't we just have fun and enjoy it?" Leaning into him, I brace both hands on his chest and nibble my way across his jaw to that tempting bottom lip.

His thoughtful expression down at me gives nothing away, but his gears are cranking.

"Tick tock, doc," I tease, "you have patients waiting."

"Don't say that." He rests his forehead to mine, trying to steady his pout. "You're not...it's not like that with you, Addison. I—"

Silencing him with a molten kiss, I scoot forward, rubbing myself across his front while I work open a few more buttons of his shirt. "Touch me...I need my doctor," I moan into his mouth, the exposed, taut muscles under my hands unfurling my passion.

"Your doctor?" he grates, pulling out of my hold and stepping back.

It's obvious he's conflicted, but I need him to see exactly what this is between us. A fantasy, playtime, never anything more.

"My doctor," I confirm resolutely.

Predatorily, he crosses the room, closing the buttons up his shirt, then turns back to me, a cloud of understanding passing between us. "Strip," he demands, his voice so low and thick it reverberates over my flesh.

I do as he says, first slipping off my shoes, then sliding my short skirt down my legs, never once breaking my eager stare from his stoic one. After I toss the thin fabric over the chair, I pull off my shirt and stand before him in black panties and matching bra.

His confidence radiates off him. "You're here for an exam aren't you, Addison?"

"Yes." I reply, willing the trembling in my legs to cease.

"Then take it all off."

I want this, more than anything, but suddenly I'm feeling on edge. He's watching me, hard eyes inspecting.

Reaching back, I unsnap my bra and let it slip down my arms. "Do you want to help with my panties?" I ask, attempting to bring back the playful doc.

"No, I'm not your boyfriend, remember, I'm your *doctor*. Take them off and turn around."

Turn around? I swallow. That was never part of his exam in the past. The look he gives silences any questions. My panties glide down my legs and I step out, tossing them aside, and timidly turn away.

Overly aware of every sound, every movement, every nerve, my anxiousness peaks. There's nothing for a long moment until I hear his footsteps, followed by the loud snap of a glove from somewhere behind me that causes a flinch I can't hide. *What the hell is he doing?*

Fingers touch my back, trail down my spine, and over the curve of my ass.

My eyes flutter shut, breath hitching. "What are you doing?" I ask, my voice a whisper.

"Inspecting."

"What exactly?"

His hands roughly grip my waist. "Are you questioning your doctor?"

My breathing rushes out in heavy pants. "No."

"Good, up on the table and lie back."

I do as he says again, nerves flipping in eager excitement. *Here we go. Back on track.*

He stands over me and places both palms over my breasts, cupping the weight in his hands. My nipples pebble, aching to be caressed, teased, and tasted.

"These are symmetric, a solid C fit for your petite frame. And your nipples…" he squeezes my right breast then lowers his head, "are deliciously perky." His moist tongue sweeps over the sensitive flesh, my eyelids heavy with my rapid intake of breath.

Leisurely, his tongue bathes my nipple with teasing licks. He's no longer gentle when he sucks it past his warm mouth, his lips closing around it as his fingers mold and knead. He takes his time, giving the utmost attention as he learns every inch. He's never focused so heavily on them before and I'm basking in it, their sensitivity riveting.

His teeth bare and more than nibble, biting my nipple, a slice of pain shooting out with my purring cry. But abruptly he pulls away, despite my lurid whimper telling him how much I'm enjoying his affection.

I want more. My pout is undeniable but short-lived as I watch the corner of his shamelessly succulent mouth lift into a knowing smirk. Unaware what to expect, I'm consumed with a sweltering shiver when he dips his head between my breasts and trails his tongue across to the other, properly greeting my left breast. A bolt of heat enflames me, commencing the drip at my center.

"No issues here," he states oh-so-formally. That's right, he's my doctor, and a damn fine one at that.

"Good to know," I say, staring at his enticing lips. I crave them, almost begging them to come to me, take mine, kiss me like no one else ever could, but I don't, because that's not what a doctor would do, and the doctor is clearly in charge today.

Instead I sit up and watch as he walks to the end of the table and pulls out the stirrups.

Yes, please.

"Scoot down. I want that ass *right here.*" He slams a hand forcefully at the end of the table.

Braced on my hands, I wiggle forward, following his directions, watching him roll over the tray of clean tools. Determination tight on his features, he sits calmly on his stool, sinister eyes tracking my movements.

Tools?

"Wait? What are you—"

"Lift your foot, Addison."

What? My body goes rigid, foot locked down on the table, forcing him to pry it up and place it in the stirrup. I fall back and allow him easier access to my other one. So far I've enjoyed his new exam technique, why should I worry now?

With both legs where he wants them, I can only see his face when he lifts his hands and removes first one glove then the other.

"How many partners have you had?" he asks in a stern doctor voice.

"Excuse me?" I sit up on my elbows, narrowed eyes cast on him.

"It's a simple question." He raises up, challenging me with his firm scrutiny. "How many cocks have you allowed in this gorgeous pussy of yours?"

I should be furious. Doctor or lover, it's none of his damn business, but the way he's staring at me, trailing his tongue over his lips when he glances back at my dripping center, I'm compelled to answer.

"Two, only two," I confess.

He places his hands on my thighs and murmurs. "Undeserving bastards. *No one* is allowed near here again."

I say nothing, stunned at his severe tone.

"Answer me. Tell me you understand."

I nod in agreement, then speak. "Yes, I understand."

This is only a game, I remind myself, *some roleplaying fun,* so I go with it. Not that there's anyone else I'm looking to entertain down there anyway.

Satisfaction carves out over his features. "Good. Now shall we continue with the exam?"

"Please, doctor."

His hands slip under my ass, his eyes gleaming in approval. "So perfect...every part of you." Caressing his fingers over my wriggling ass, he trails them under my legs then leans forward and traces his tongue down my inner thigh until his nose brushes my sex, then stops and moves back.

My body trembling in need, I watch as he removes the speculum from the tray and looks to me.

"No need for lubrication this time. You're soaking wet."

"I know," I reply brazenly.

His lip quirks up but it's gone instantly as he settles back on his stool and the cool metal pokes at my sex.

Anticipation rushes over me in fiery waves. I wait for him to slide it in but it never comes. Instead he strokes it up and down against my searing, drenched flesh, teasing me, taunting me. A moan spills out, louder than appropriate and his hands abruptly still.

"If a single nurse hears your moans…" The speculum presses down against my aching clit. I arch my back off the bed, grinding my hips upward, searching for friction against the smooth metal. "Then I'll fuck you with this instead of my mouth."

It presses harder, then in a wicked move he slides it down and slips it inside me, stretching me as his head dips and tongue flicks my pulsating bud once, then twice, in another tease.

"Which do you prefer?" His tongue strokes me again and mixed with the pressure of being stretched, I babble, lost in want.

"Tongue, both, please, you."

"Maybe you'd prefer my fingers inside you again instead?" He removes the tool and the loud thud it makes when he tosses it back on the tray echoes off the wall.

I can barely focus as his thumb is still swirling over my clit. I feel two fingers sliding over my mound, spreading my juices over my entire sex. Biting my lip, I quiver violently, body moist with sweat. His thumb draws back and my swollen clit aches for more.

"Mmmmm," he moans, followed by the sounds of his lips smacking shut. Did he just lick his fingers?"

I can't stop writhing, breathing hard, wanting to see him. Sitting up, I reach for him but am met with a gentle hand pushing me back down.

"I said lay back. Unless you want to end the exam?" The deep command in his murmur holds my focus. All I can see are his dark, clouded eyes gauging me.

"N-no. Don't stop. Please, I need more."

"Anticipation is one of life's greatest pleasures. Now let me do my job properly."

Staring up at the ceiling, immersed in pleasure, I feel his fingers spread me wider, opening my lower lips. Anticipation is an understatement; I'm about to burst into flames without his touch where I need it most.

His hands move to each of my thighs and in one long

lap, his tongue runs over the entire length of my slit. I cry out, placing my hand over my mouth to silence the sobs of pleasure as he delves his tongue deep.

This is where you need a real sheet under you to grip onto, not a paper one that shreds in your hands. Still, I claw at it, arching up into his mouth as he caresses my inner walls. I've hardly had my fill when his tongue flicks out and sets its beautiful torture to my clit, two fingers satisfying my neglected center.

They thrust in and out, hooking up and hitting the exact spot they seek, the spot no man has touched in me before. My screams spill against my palms, covering my mouth as I writhe and buck against him.

His face is buried between my legs as he inserts a third finger, which stretches me in pure delight. I shudder and convulse, my walls gripped around his digits as I buck up once more. As the wave washes me away, I fall back, oblivious to all but sheer bliss.

His fingers fall away and he stands. I sit up, catching my breath, still dizzy from my orgasm but ready for his dick to fill me. When I reach out to him he steps back and walks over to the sink.

I watch, unsure what to think when he pumps two squirts of soap on his hands and washes them hastily.

Once he grabs a paper towel, he turns back to me, face passive.

My lips curl up, legs falling open in the stirrups. "It's your turn to strip," I hum.

"Why would I do that?" he asks, tossing the towel in the trash can and crossing his arms over his chest.

I blanch at the harshness in his tone. "What? I thought…I mean…I want you. I want to feel you inside me."

"You just had my fingers and my tongue, what else do you want?" He's goading me to say it. I'll play along if he needs to hear it.

I sit up straighter and lean forward, palms down against the table supporting me. "I *want* your cock."

"Hmm, well problem with that is," he stalks towards me, stopping inches from my face, "I don't *fuck* my patients." With that, he turns on his heel and storms from the room, leaving me rooted in place, feeling anything but satisfied.

Chapter Fourteen

I leave Dr. Reynolds' office unsure what to make of his last words. Unlike the previous times he'd left the room after our trysts, I was never regarded so severely. I drive straight home, my thoughts muddled, ready to soak in a hot bath to clear my head then curl up on the couch for a marathon of my favorite sitcom. Jack and Karen usually never fail at having me doubled over in fits of hysterics, no matter how many times I've seen the episode, but tonight I barely crack a smile.

Something changed between us and I have a feeling his secretary won't be calling tomorrow. Shifting the pillow under my back, I brush off the looming chance that our scandalous rendezvous could be ending and gulp down another swig of wine. He just needs time to see what we have is ideal—no fuss, no strings, simply raw pleasure.

I refuse to worry over what the future may bring and enjoy the mental replay of his hands working over my chest, the pressure of his fingers, the smoldering desire in his blatant stare. My eye slide shut and I'm there again, relishing the roughness of his words, a molten zing coursing through me from his vulgar, dominating instructions.

Of course I can't stay in that happy place for long as my phone begins to buzz from the side table. No clue who would be calling, I'm pleasantly surprised to see Dylan's name on the screen, half wondering if he might have butt dialed.

"Guess I can call off the APB," I greet him.

"Mocifus! How the hell are ya?"

"Pretty good. What about you? I feel like we haven't talked in forever." I slink back in the sofa with my glass.

"We haven't." He laughs. "Sorry about that, I've just been busy getting things up and running."

My smile can't be contained—my brother's actually living his dream! "Don't apologize, Dyl. I'm so proud and excited for you!"

"Thanks," he says, his voice humble. "So hey, can you do lunch tomorrow, my treat?"

"Of course! Need my big brother fix."

"Great, say noon at Ruby's?"

I immediately agree and end the call with a giddy excitement, sitting back a minute to revel in how happy I am for my brother.

I'M ACTUALLY more surprised that I'm surprised...why *wouldn't* Brady be here, already seated and cutting up with Dylan as I'm lead to their table?

"There she is!" Dylan springs from his seat to wrap me in an energetic embrace. "You look great, Moe. I've missed you."

"Me too." Swiping quickly at my silly tears of pride, I glance hesitantly at Brady, who still hasn't greeted me as Dylan pushes in my chair. It's official. "Brady and Moe" is broken. Never has that man not acknowledged me within five seconds of being in a room. For fuck's sake! I didn't say we couldn't talk, I said we couldn't be more. But in all fairness, I haven't gone out of my way to send a text and invite him over to hang out either. It's no longer easy with us as friends and I haven't been able to bring myself to face it.

Seems his "coward" comment held more truth than I'd care to admit.

"Hello, Brady," I grind out as civilly as possible, aggravated at his stubbornness.

"Moe." He gives a curt nod.

Dylan's watching back and forth like a Ping-Pong match, understandably confused. "The hell? Ya'll have a fight?"

Brady cocks one brow my way, challenging me to answer. Not biting. "No, of course not." I smile at Dyl. "Anyway, this is your day. So tell us all about things."

Don't have to ask him twice; he instantly starts gushing out all that's been happening as I hold my enthusiastic smile firmly in place, trying to keep up and stay focused, while kicking Brady under the table. He looks my way only once and I stick out my tongue, face twisted up like a slapstick comic seeking a laugh. I don't get one and when I kick my foot out again its only air I hit; he's moved his leg, and worse, he's scooting his chair over.

Thankfully, Ruby's is a sandwich shop, so we're able to order and be served quickly, the atmosphere slightly more amicable, but still "off" despite my attempts to lighten his mood. Brady wasn't this quiet when he had laryngitis two years ago, and if he doesn't stop dampening Dylan's parade with his pouting, I *will* throw this pickle at him.

"So you'll both come, right?"

"What?" I ask, having zoned out on the last part of Dylan's speech.

His head cranes my way. "My launch party. It's this Friday night. You'll be there?"

"Of course I will." I pat his jittery hand. "Wouldn't miss it for the world. Just let me know when and where. Did I mention how proud of you I am?"

"Shucks, ma'am," he jests with a wave of his hand. "Oh and it's formal, so gown and tux," he speaks between us both. "And bring dates. The more the merrier. I want a big crowd there."

I struggle to temper my expression—formal *and* a date, not what I'd expect from my brother.

"You got it. No worries," Brady says directly to Dylan. His voice cuts through me, sparking the flame Dr. Reynolds had been managing.

We're mercifully saved from further "surprises" by Dylan's phone, but the bomb's already dropped...gown and date.

"Sorry guys, but I need to go. See you Friday?" My brother leans down and kisses my cheek, hardly waiting for our answers before he's out the door.

I jump up, busying myself with throwing away our trash, ready to rush out as well. But as I turn I'm immediately pinned by a brooding, menacing Brady hovering in my space.

"Be my date for Dylan's party, Moe. Me and you, please. I miss *us*."

"Do you?" I scoff, shoving against his chest, not budging him whatsoever. "Could've fooled me! What's with the doom and gloom pouting then? You could have gotten up and hugged me, called me, anything! Didn't seem like you missed us? Which, P.S., is *exactly* the reason I said no to more in the first place!"

"Well excuse the fuck outa me! It's not easy to figure

out the rules—*your* rules! I could have sworn there was something real here, Moe, so I put myself out there and you basically shot me down, right through the heart! *P.S.* maybe I can't snap back into 'just friends' mode like you can. Maybe I wanna sit beside you and caress your back or—ahh!" He mocks a gasp. "Maybe I want to hold your little hand, no matter where we are or who's watching." His tone drops along with his face, anger suddenly morphed into hurt. "I just…I could've sworn you thought Brady and Moe was something different now too."

Lowering my head on a sigh, I fight the anguished quivering in my chin. I never want to see him hurt and I never meant to cause it. "Listen, Brady, you're my best friend and I miss you desperately but I've got something—" I stop, not wanting to delve into things in the middle of Ruby's.

"Be. My. Date," he growls lowly in my face.

My head's shaking before I refuse verbally and he's once again already sulking out, nearly ripping the door off when he shoves it open. I hate myself in this moment. My head falls back against the wall, my arms wrapping around myself, wanting to hide from the world. I don't even notice the tears until a voice asks, "You okay, Miss?"

I look up to find a waitress staring at me with nothing but pity. With an irate huff, I push off the wall. "Golden."

It's me that's busting out their door next, ready to crawl back in bed and end this damn day.

<hr>

A DRESS? You'd think that'd be simple enough to find, except I've been to half the shops in town and found not one. It isn't helping that the event is tomorrow, and after spending the last few days going from work to home and straight to bed, I'm quickly running out of time and options.

Maybe I'm depressed, which seems ridiculous to me because only a few days earlier I was damn near giddy with the hand I'd been dealt—deliciously erotic doctor appointments—and now... Now everything is as fucked up as my dress hunt.

I need something that reflects the love and pride I have for Dylan. I'm standing in the last shop in town, begging the universe to show some mercy, when it does just that. I snatch the dress from the rack with a triumphant smile. It has a babydoll-style skirt, corseted waist, and plunging neckline in a gorgeous off-white with just a hint of silver highlighted throughout. It's even more gorgeous when I see the price tag; I can afford new heels to match.

I head straight to the dressing room hoping it looks as good on me as it does the hanger when I hear my name.

"Addison?"

I turn toward the unfamiliar voice and see the brainy beauty, aka Brady's last date, standing with a long gown in hand. Crap, what's her name?

"Hi." I grin a bit too much hoping it will cover the nameless slip.

"You don't remember me?" She laughs softly, almost like music. No wonder Brady asked her out.

"No, I do! Brady brought you to dinner," I say quickly, then confess. "Sorry, I'm horrible with names. It's nothing personal."

"It's Ashley and don't worry about it, I forget all the time."

"Right, sorry, but you remembered mine, which means you're just being polite right now or I left a memorable impression." I pale as the words fall out, remembering why she'd have a lasting impression of me after my abrupt exit that night. "Look, sorry I up and left during the dinner, it's just…"

"You don't have to explain. And the reason I remember you so well is because Brady talks about you often. You two seem like close friends."

My shoulders drop. "Yeah." It's barely a whisper.

"Love the dress. It's gorgeous. I almost grabbed it for myself." She nudges her head at my hands gripping the fabric.

"Thanks, you found a good choice…classic black." The dress draped over her arm is long and screams graceful and timeless. "What's the occasion?"

"I'm guessing same as you. Dylan's party tomorrow night."

It's a surreal moment, the kind where the air is ripped painfully from your lungs and you don't know whether to laugh or cry. With a spinning head and failing knees, I could swear an earthquake is pulsing under my feet.

She's going to the party, which means Brady found a date. I retreat into the dressing room before I lose my sense in front of her and say something I'll regret. They'll look good together. Brady in a tux, her corralled in his arms...I can't stomach the thought.

"Well, I guess I'll see you there," I say in an awkward huff, then quickly shut the dressing room door.

"Okay, yeah, bye," I hear her say but I'm already squatted down on the floor, face in my hands, trying to block out the assaulting images of her and Brady together.

He deserves to be happy, I remind myself. I have to let him go, let him take the time he needs to be angry at me. Eventually he'll see that "we" are too important to risk on a tryst. There can never be more, despite the flicker of hope and tearful musings of how extraordinary "more" would probably be warming my chest.

Chapter Fifteen

I'M LATE. Only by five minutes or so, but still late to the most important night of my brother's life. Guilt eats at me yet does little to quicken my pace.

My excuse, in case he notices, is still being debated. Traffic is always a safe bet but in reality the only thing to blame is my own selfish procrastination.

I dragged ass from the moment I got off work. I watched a little television, painted my nails only to remove it and repaint them a different color, and *then* finally hauled myself into the bathroom to get ready an hour before the event began.

So here I am, stepping into a grand hotel in the center of town, reluctant to pass through the double doors leading to the ballroom.

And no, my tardiness has nothing to do with the fact that I know I'll find a gorgeous Brady on the other side, charming the room with a flawless date wrapped around his arm.

Nope, nothing at all.

I hope he is in there; happy, carefree, wearing his usual smug grin, back to his old self. Truly.

I check my coat and square my shoulders, ready to do nothing but celebrate my brother's accomplishment. He has a lot of work to do to the get the business off the ground, but tonight it's official, he's putting the pieces together to bring it to life.

Seems lots of things are changing.

A waiter greets me, handing me a glass of champagne, then steps aside, revealing the room awaiting me.

The quick chug I take of the liquid bravado nearly sputters out as I take in the insanely stunning scenery, decorated in white linens and Dylan's black "Game On!" logo. The atmosphere leaves me breathless. Never would I have thought it could look so chic. Dylan knows games, but throwing a party? *He must've found an incredible planner.*

Time to go find my big bro and remind him just how amazing he is.

Once I'm fully immersed in the room, I spot Dylan near the band and my face splits into a wide grin. Eager to get to his side where I plan to remain all night, I weave through the crowd of mingling guests, but as I draw closer, my feet trip me up in an abrupt stop. Dylan's in deep conversation with not just two studious men whom I've never seen before, but also Ashley, who's looking as beautiful as I knew she would.

Brady's not with them, but he can't be far. He wouldn't leave his date alone with all these men, not with the way she fills out that dress. I snatch another glass of champagne from a passing tray and gulp.

Feeling out of place, I move back, unsure if I should wait until she leaves his side or go say hi now. It's silly and ridiculous. He's *my* brother, but still, I don't want Dylan to see any awkwardness tonight.

Deciding I'll bide my time before I say hello, I stand there alone and unnatural, wishing I had brought a date. As

I try to block out my solo status, a current of electricity sizzles down the back of my neck. I don't need to turn around to know he's here. He's close. I can feel him behind me, my body hyperaware of him tonight.

I wait, expecting him to speak or step around me to say hello when I feel his breath hit the back of my ear, caressing it. *Damn him*. Friends! Friends!

And then he surprises me yet again when he slips past me, his arm brushing mine as strides smoothly over to his date waiting beside Dylan. She welcomes him over with a sweet smile.

Brady doesn't look at me once he's there in the small group, laughing and chatting it up, so I decide to make the most of my night and walk up to the first guy I see standing alone.

"Hi," I say cheerfully. "I'm Addison Porter, Dylan's sister. Nice to meet you."

The guy looks to be around Dylan and Brady's age; not as built, but cute. His hair is dark and neatly trimmed, no facial hair and dull brown eyes but still…cute.

He gives me a noticeable once over before his lips curl up and he takes my hand, giving it a gentle squeeze.

"Pleasure. I'm Cole. Friends with Dylan for a few years now. Good guy."

Dylan has very few friends and none I've never meant unless he means… "Online gaming friends?" I ask, curious.

He nods with a hint of embarrassment in his smile. "Yeah, I know it's not the sexiest thing. Most girls hate guys that game, but it's in my blood. I flew out tonight to show my support."

"Addison." I look up to see my brother and Brady walking over, Brady's eyes hard and zoomed in on Cole.

What provokes me, I haven't a clue, but I tug my lip between my teeth and lean in and whisper to Cole, "I think it's kind of sexy."

"What's sexy?" Dylan asks, standing beside me now.

"Uh, nothing. Hey, sorry I didn't come over yet, I just got here and you looked busy." I give him a quick hug. "I love you. I can't tell you how impressed I am. And how—"

"Proud you are," he finishes for me with a chuckle as he releases me. "I know and I've been hearing it all night from Mom and Dad too, who are looking for you, by the way."

"Cole!" Dylan turns his attention to his cyber buddy,

leaving me and Brady standing beside each other.

I steal an uncomfortable glance his way just as Ashley appears at his side.

"Gotta say, never would have believed it if I wasn't seeing it." Cole laughs, slapping Dylan on the back. "You, of all people, about to run a business."

"My brother's one of the best gamers out there," I defend him instantly, earning me a bashful look from Dylan.

Cole drinks me in. "No doubt about that. But this party—I wasn't expecting it to be so formal, so put together," he clarifies.

"Oh." I slink back, lowering my head. "Yeah, it's gorgeous."

"Can't take the credit for that. It was all Ashley over here." Dylan nudges his head her way.

Of course she put the party together, she's superwoman, after all.

Ashley takes the compliment with easy poise then excuses herself to the ladies' room. Dylan retreats a moment later to go mingle, leaving Brady and Cole standing around me.

One peek at each of them confirms that the "sizing up the competition" thing men do is in play, which is absolutely ridiculous.

"Ashley looks beautiful tonight," I say to Brady.

His brows pinch. "She does."

Cole moves closer to me. "Lucky man. How long have you and her been together?" he asks Brady.

Yeah, Brady? How long? Has he been stringing her along this whole time? My temper peeks at the unpleasant pang of jealousy that flares.

"We're—"

I can't bear to hear his answer so I cut in. "She's good for you. I like her."

His eyes darken at my words then narrow a moment later when Cole's hand slides around my waist. I don't push him away, instead allowing the touch from a total stranger.

Cole pulls me closer. "You wanna dance?"

My eyes on Brady, I'm conflicted on how to answer. I don't want to hurt my best friend, but he's here with someone else, which means whatever he felt for me obviously wasn't that strong. Our friendship will rebound and maybe seeing me with someone else will help put things back into perspective for him. I'm not his.

"You should probably go check on Ashley," I say over the music, "in case she needs your help or something. I'm good here."

I don't give him a chance to reply. Cole takes my hand and leads me out onto the dance floor where he wraps his arms around my back, holding me close.

Leave it to Brady to deal with things in a mature, classy manner.

Or not.

Apparently Ashley rebuffed his plans or wasn't fast enough in the ladies' room, so he's now latched and I do mean *latched*, on to the tackiest bimbo in the room. Rolling my eyes and pulling Cole closer against my body, I try *not* to steal glances over his shoulder at Brady's antics, but sometimes, like a car wreck, you just have to look.

And when I do, his mouth may be on her neck, his hands groping her ass in true porn fashion, but his eyes…they're on me. Hard, determined, and challenging, he glares my way but why I'm—for once—not sure.

Is he begging me to pull him off her or outdo his brazenness with my current partner?

Is he pissed off?

I can't pull my eyes away despite Cole's whispering in my ear, which is incoherent since my brain is busily processing the sight that's crippling me with emotions I can't squash.

As Brady's fingers tighten and knead her tiny ass, he rolls his hips, pressing his pelvis into her—I have my answer. My brows raise, telling him I won't back down.

Challenge accepted!

My hand slips down from Cole's shoulder and grips the hem of my dress, hitching it up just enough to slide my leg higher up Cole's hip. I dip my head back, my chest pushing forward, and giggle at nothing, praying Brady can hear it above the music.

A deep, low growl escaping Cole freezes me in place and I fight from recoiling at the thick length hardening against my stomach.

"So fine," he whispers.

I place my hands tighter against his shoulders and pull myself back into our previous, normal dancing position. That should be enough to show Brady two can play that game.

Ashamed for involving Cole, I give him a sweet smile then chance a peek to assess Brady's reaction and the saying holds true—play with fire and you will get burned.

Which I am, scorching from head to toe in a blaze of excruciating fury as I watch Brady dip the hussy and feed feverishly at her mouth. When he pulls her back up and links his fingers with hers, the motherfucker *winks at me* while he whispers in her ear, then, to my horror, leads her off the dance floor.

I'm frozen in agony, each of their steps leading to the double doors where their sordid tryst awaits sending a splinter of jealous agony through me till my gut is twisted beyond repair, about to explode.

"Mmm, come back here," Cole grunts in my ear.

I robotically push him away, eyes still on that damn door. Brady turns back once and catches my stare, a passing flash of I can't decipher what it is on his face before he turns and continues his exit...officially taking what I thought was a bratty game of torment way too far.

"Mind if I cut in?" my father asks, appearing out of nowhere.

Cole looks to me with guarded restraint. I've definitely

led him on tonight, but the fury flooding my veins keeps me from feeling the depths of the guilt. I'll simply add it to my recent list of sins as I never plan to see the man again.

"Of course not, Dad." I force a smile his way then press myself closer to Cole for a brief hug and whisper, "Thanks for the dance." I place a chaste kiss to his cheek then turn and take my father's hand.

Cole leaves the dance floor, seemingly satisfied, after throwing me a subtle wave. It eases a tinge of the rage I have when I glance at the door again.

Just like when I was a young girl, my father twirls me out then draws me back into his arms. I smile for him, always daddy's little girl, but the thought of Brady out there somewhere with that…my lip trembles.

My head rests against my father's shoulder as I blink back tears.

"You look beautiful tonight, baby girl."

"Thank you, Daddy." I swallow past the knot in my throat. "Can you believe it? Dyl's really doing it."

"Yeah, we always knew he'd find his way, just like you did."

"Right." *My way?* Had I found it? Sure doesn't feel like

it.

"Is something wrong?" He pulls his head back and I lift mine, his lowered brows pressing me to talk.

"I'm just a little lost right now, that's all," I confess, shuffling my feet, constantly glancing to the infuriating door Brady has yet to reenter.

"Is this about Brady?"

My breath catches and I shake my head with adamant denial. "No, Brady and I are fine." My lie is smooth.

"Good." He looks relieved but it doesn't last. "You'd tell us if there was something wrong, right?" he asks, twirling me out again.

"Yeah, of course."

He's staring down at me as though he's waiting for something, for me to spill some big secret. What exactly does he know? Did Brady talk to Dylan? Or someone else? It's a small town, after all. I'm not sure what to say.

"Addison, honey, it's none of my business and you'd probably prefer to talk to your mother about it but…" His voice lowers and a hint of a blush creeps over his cheeks, one that I haven't seen since he attempted the birds and the bees talk when I was fourteen. "There's been some talk around town and I'm worried."

"Talk? About what?" The song winds down and I step out of his arms, suddenly apprehensive at the way his face tightens with worry. Dad's always loved Brady like a son; I know he'd be thrilled for us to get together and wouldn't understand my refusal. My head's a wreck, forming a drawn out explanation why Brady and I are better as friends.

"That you've been to doctor's office a lot lately. If there's something you need to tell us, please, we're here for you. Whatever it is, we'll get through it."

Get through it? Get through what? Then it hits me. He thinks I'm sick. It has nothing to do with Brady. It's about all my appointments.

I laugh, almost manically so, until his worry turns into horror at my outburst. It's official—my life can get no worse.

"Addison!" my mother calls out, stepping beside us.

"Mom, hi." I embrace her, shushing my chuckle.

"I told you not to say anything to her tonight," she chastises my father in a whisper.

"If my daughter's sick I want to know it!" he retorts.

They lock eyes, a discussion with no words being held

between them. I've seen it before; they rarely fight, just exchange looks that put issues to rest, but tonight it baffles me.

"When you're ready to talk to us, we'll be there to listen," my mother says to me.

My father wraps an arm around her waist and kisses her hair; I have to smother a sigh at their easy comfort with each other.

"How do you do it?" I ask. I've never questioned their relationship before, but I need to understand why some people have it so easy.

"Do what, honey?" my father asks.

"You never fight. You're always affectionate, still stealing kisses after all these years. How do you do it? How does it work so well for you?" *But not me* I want to add but don't.

"That's simple," my mother starts then looks up to my father to finish.

"I married my best friend," he says.

My mother snuggles him closer, nodding her head.

Best friends. I swallow hard, a tight smile forming to appease them, but it's filled with sadness and before I can help it, my chin starts quivering, my eyes prickling with tears.

My head bounces in understanding. "I need some air. Excuse me." I back away and turn quickly, pushing through the guests littering the dance floor searching for an escape.

My mother's voice calls my name but I don't stop, rushing my steps, shouldering people aside until I realize there's only one escape and I refuse to run into Brady macking on some bimbo. I can't handle it.

Darting my head back and forth, I'm granted a moment of mercy when I spot an exit sign glaring along the back wall. I nearly sprint toward it as imagines of Brady kissing her, sliding his hands under that skimpy dress riddle my flustered mind. I tug at my necklace, now choking me, suffocating me. I desperately need air.

It's not just Brady I picture, but Dr. Reynolds now too, groping her in his office, spreading her legs in his stirrups. She's probably his patient, after all. It's all some bad joke.

I knock over a poor waiter, champagne flutes flying off his tray and shattering on the ground, spraying guests with the bubbling liquid. A quick "sorry" is all I can offer, though. I'm too close to freedom to stop.

I spot Ashley beside my brother, laughing at something he's saying. She's a sweet girl; I feel bad that she fell for Brady's charm. I wonder if she spent any time looking for him when she came out of the ladies' room. Brady's a jerk, I'm a jerk and this whole mess is deserved.

My palms slam open the doors and I suck in a deep lungful of cool night air. I'm standing on a gated alcove covered with a massive awning overhead with no guests around, nothing but one dying light hanging down. I welcome the darkness. It suits my mood.

Clawing at the back of my neck, unable to remove my damn necklace, my sobs begin to spill out. "Dammit!"

"Shh." A gentle voice caresses my back as do strong hands that move mine away to easily unclasp the jewelry. It's Brady that steps around me and places it in my hand, but I already knew at first touch that it was him.

"That was quick!" I snarl, stumbling back, swiping angrily at my damn tears. "Where'd you fuck her? In the parking lot?" My laugh is harsh, cruel even to my own ears. With a sinister sneer, I step back into him. "You're such a goddamn prick!"

"Is that so?" His voice is steady, indifferent. Nothing but a cool façade, albeit his glittering eyes that sheen with something else.

"Yes! Yes, it is so. Why even bring a date if you were going to screw around, huh? You just don't care who you hurt!"

His arms fly out to the sides, teeth bearing with his roar. "Oh, I care! I care too damn much! It's you that's heartless."

I recoil at his tone. "Heartless?" I breathe.

When he takes a step closer, the dim light highlights the sharpness of his tense features. "I didn't bring a date tonight. I asked the only girl I wanted here with me and she turned me down. Like she always does."

I shake my head. "No, no you brought Ashley. You wanted to make me jealous and—"

"And it did," he finishes.

My head shakes violently this time. "I was just angry that you were ignoring me. Not jealous. We're friends, Brady. I want to see you happy. If Ashley makes you—"

"She's not my fucking date!" He grabs my forearms as

if to shake me but holds me firmly in place. "Do you hear me? She's here with Dylan."

"What?!"

His grip tightens and I can't ignore the way his fingers press into my chilled flesh. "If you got out of your own fucking head, you'd see that Dylan's crazy about her. She was never anything but a friend and if you knew me like you think you do then you'd *know that*."

"She's beautiful...smart."

"No comparison. You're everything, Moe." His head dips, mouth skimming my ear. "Come home with me."

I inhale his scent, my hands clinging to his jacket, when I'm hit with the smell of cheap peaches, his dance partner's perfume who he just—

I shove him away. "Get off me. Let go!"

He does so immediately, his voice and expression arctic. "No more excuses!"

"Excuses? You just screwed some nobody just to piss me off! You really think I'd want anything to do with you after that?"

Brady's noticeably affected, his hands clenched at his sides, nerve in his clenched jaw twitching. He looks past me with an anguished sigh. "Explain to me what you really want. Please. Just some trashy affair with your doctor?"

"Don't!" My voice squeaks, no idea what more to say, how to explain what I feel in Dr. Reynolds' office. But I know it isn't fair to Brady. He wants more, needs more, and I can't give it.

"What? You think you can go in that office whenever you have an itch and no one will be affected? No one will gossip? This is a small town, Moe."

"I'm not talking about it." I can't. It was just fun. Dr. Reynolds allowed me to live a fantasy, one that I refuse to regret.

"Fine, then answer me one question, and I'll walk away. You won't have to worry about dealing with me again."

The thought of him leaving damn near breaks me, but I hold firm.

He stands in front of me, wary vulnerability in his eyes. "Tell me the truth. Tell me why, despite our attraction for each other, you won't let us be happy. Because, babe, I would do anything for you. I'd make you the happiest woman alive if you'd let me." His hand moves to my cheek, thumb brushing over my trembling bottom lip. "Tell me why you're pushing me away."

I close my eyes, unable to look at him as I answer. "Because I need my best friend and if we don't work out, I can't risk losing you forever."

Eyes still shut, his hand drops away and I feel him move back. "It's too late. You've already lost me."

I open my eyes, watching him start through the side gate. He doesn't look back, but I hear him clearly. "And if you really think I slept with that girl, you never knew me at all."

There's nothing for me to say. I stand there, tears spilling out, arms crossed over my chest, holding myself together while I watch him walk further into the darkness.

My chest constricts, something shattering deep inside at the thought of never seeing Brady again, of never laughing or joking with him, never holding him close. I lose myself in the grief, sinking down to the ground where I deserve to be. I screwed up. I lost the only man I can't bear to live without.

Chapter Sixteen

EVERYONE gets their fifteen minutes of fame, right?

Well, mine are up. For a brief blip of time I'd felt special, amazing, alive…and just as quickly, it's over.

I sold my soul to the devil—the snarling beast awakened inside me—for a few visits with a "happy ending." Now I'm left a shell of myself. An empty, hollow ache in my chest, rats in my hair, and stains on my three day old pajamas.

After the fifth time I was told, "His schedule is full," I quit trying to make an appointment with Dr. Reynolds.

After the seventh failed rendezvous with my almost

forgotten little blue friend, I threw it away.

And Brady...

I miss him like fat kids—which I'll soon be if I don't snap out of this funk—miss cake. Speaking of cake... I rouse my dumpy, frumpy self off the couch, pausing my *Will and Grace* DVD, to shuffle into the kitchen.

Knowing I'll regret it later, I plunge my fork into what's left of my beloved turtle cheesecake. My eyes close, delighting in the cool and creamy sweetness.

Brady hates caramel, so I always make sure I have one with cherry topping for him...

Stop it!

Slamming the licked clean fork down on the counter, sick of myself, I almost don't pick out the knock on my door from the sound of my own admonishment. Another knock echoes and I twist back to stare at the door, painfully aware I'm in no way ready to greet visitors. One look around the room says my home isn't either.

I wonder if I can hire Kathy to at least pull my apartment back together when my pity party ends.

Smoothing my tousled hair, I duck to catch my reflection in the small mirror by the door. Oh hell! I grab a baseball cap from the rack and as I'm about to shove it on to cover my mess, I stop. It's Brady's cap. He must have left it here…God knows when.

My fingers run over the brim and before I can stop myself, I fling it across the room and grab a thick wool cap instead. Who cares if I look like an escaped mental patient? I'm feeling a little mental.

One more peek in the mirror, wiping my face, I open the door.

There's nobody there. I poke my head further out, looking left then right and nothing. *Thank God.* I'd gear up to scream at the neighborhood kids for ding-dong ditching if there wasn't an enormous box at my feet.

I didn't order anything, let alone something in a box bigger than me! With a series of grunts and shoves, I finally manage to maneuver the monstrosity inside and rip into it. When that gets me nowhere, I run to the kitchen and grab the scissors, then try again.

I cut the last strap and fall back at the same time the box flies open, revealing the one thing I can't bear.

Holy—I am a piece of—shit.

There on my floor, wrapped in thin foam paper, is the

outline of a surfboard. Crawling over, I pull away the packaging and run my fingers over the smooth polished wood with a pink hue, my favorite color. At the top right side is a huge white lily, my middle name, under that "My Moe" in fancy black script.

I glance up at the hook where my keys hang. The keychain he brought me from California, a hint I never realized. *He had a surfboard made for me.*

Fighting back the tears, I prop the unbelievable gift against the wall, making room to clean up the box mess when I spot the card taped to the bottom side.

My hands tremble as I open it, the gravity hitting me full force—these will be the only words I've heard from Brady in over a week.

Can't wait to get you on the water with me!

Love always,

Brady

The floodgates burst wide open and fat crocodile tears roll down my cheeks, a bittersweet mixture of happiness, love, regret and loneliness. I leap up from the mushy puddle I've become on the floor and grab my phone.

I don't hesitate, my fingers typing in a flurry of

anxiousness.

Me: I got the surfboard. Thank u so much! I love it! When can we go?

Each minute that ticks by without a response cuts a little deeper into my soul and I sink down into the couch. He ordered it before everything went to shit, but now it's here, and I pray it serves as a reminder to us both of what we are and how badly we need to get back there.

Finally my phone dings, just as I was beginning to think I really had lost him forever. Hope, that amazing, beautiful swell of my heart, brings a smile to my lips.

Brady: I'm glad u like it. You're welcome. Find someone to enjoy it with.

The phone drops from my fingers. I don't want to learn to surf with "someone." I want to go with the wonderful man, my friend, who bought it for me! The longer I sit staring at my knees tucked up against my chest, the angrier I grow. At the situation, at myself, at Brady for being so damn stubborn.

I snatch the phone back up and pound the keys.

Me: If u didn't want to take me why'd u buy it?

This time he answers back right away. I know him,

despite what he thinks, I do! He was just waiting, fingers poised, itching for a comeback.

Brady: Things change. U called the shots. GTG.

I throw out my leg and kick the coffee table in anger. *Eerrr*, that impossible man! Wincing, I cradle my foot, my head hanging back. At least the physical pain matches the emotional now.

Is this worth it? Suppose Brady and I did try "more" and it doesn't work out? The backlash couldn't possibly be worse than this, right?

Too frustrated to think about it any longer, I hit play, resuming my show. I'm slumped even further down in the couch, arms crossed, my toe throbbing, when the bantering on screen catches my full attention—that's it!

Brilliant. Thank you, sitcom gods, for the enlightenment.

Determination sets in, my mind made up. I know what I have to do.

WHEN THE NURSE shuts the door behind me—thank heavens she doesn't work in the ER, clearly not quick on the uptake—I pull out my compact, checking my disguise one last time.

Wig in place. Check.

Big, black sunglasses. Check.

And now, I wait.

Shortly after, a quick knock raps on the door.

"Come in," I say in my new covert voice. It's a high-pitched mousy tone, but it works. I think so, anyway.

I'm on the table, fully dressed, when Dr. Reynolds steps in, usual devastating smile in place, spoiled by the dark circles under his sullen eyes, a scruffy jawline and wrinkled shirt.

He looks as hellish and out of sorts as I feel and a glimmer of hopefulness moves through me. Has he been miserable too?

"Good afternoon Miss, uh…" He consults his chart once more, then ever so slowly looks up at me. A smirk hints at his luscious mouth, a slight twinkle building in those sad eyes. "Ms. Beaverhousen, is it?"

"Yes, that's right. Thank you for seeing me," I say in my fake voice then move in for the kill. "A friend of mine, Addison Porter, said she called several times and couldn't get in, so I was surprised how easy it was for me."

"I can't discuss other patients, I'm sorry. So tell me, *Ms. Beaverhousen,* what can I do for you today?"

We face off, both crossing our arms defensively across our chests, waiting in tense silence for the other to cave.

Mentally, I'd been fully prepared to march in here in raging bitch mode and tell him off for ignoring me. But now that he's in front of me, looking as distraught and devastated as I've been, my heart makes other plans.

Unable to wait another minute, I pull off my sunglasses and wig, offering a sheepish grin. "Hey."

He feigns shock, clutching his chest dramatically. "Addison! It's you!"

"Oh, stop, I know you knew." My voice drops, shaking with vulnerability. "Why wouldn't you see me?"

He sits the chart down and tilts his head. "You know why."

I nod. I do know why, but held out hope he'd take my sudden appearance in his office with a bit less annoyance. Senseless or not, I'd longed for him to grab snatch me up, hold me in his arms, and tell me everything would be alright. But he says nothing else, defiant in his stance, eyes cold and hard, pinning me in place.

217

"I miss you," I choke out in a pleading whisper.

With only one step closer, still too far away, he sighs and runs a hand down his face. "I miss you too."

My head pops up, optimism piquing, a smile about to emerge, when he cuts it short.

"But not enough to continue with silly, unprofessional escapades that cheapen what I want with you."

I agree. Time to show him. "Come here." I crook my finger to beckon him closer.

"Addison," he grumbles his warning but does, in fact, move to me a moment later. "What do you want from me?" His hot breath fans over my face, tickling my lips severely testing my resolve.

"A date," I say with conviction.

His eyes search mine with trepidation, gauging my sincerity, obviously finding what they seek as a brilliant, wickedly beautiful grin lights up his face. "Yeah?"

"Yeah."

"Hmm, what did you have in mind?" Finally he touches me, an innocent caress over my knuckles, speaking volumes.

"I want to cook you one of my specialties."

His other hand brushes over my cheek. "Is that so?"

"Mhhm. Then I thought we could cuddle on my couch and watch a movie."

"I'd like that," he says head dipping to mine.

"Me too." As hard as it is, I duck down and slink off the exam table.

He turns to me, watching as I grab my wig, twisting up my ponytail and pulling it back on then snatch my sunglasses.

"My place, tonight. Eightish?" I say, desperately wanting to kiss him but feeling the overwhelming need to wait, to give him a real date first. I slide on my sunglasses.

"Eightish," he confirms, then walks over and startles me. I think he's going to take my face in his hands, but instead he places them on the wig, adjusting it slightly. He leans down and presses a kiss to my cheek. "See you then, Ms. Beaverhousen."

AT EIGHT O'CLOCK sharp, there's a rasp on my door and I hastily straighten my hair and outfit, suppressing a giggle as I go to answer it.

"Well, hello," I coo. "How lucky am I to have a doctor

that makes house calls!"

A frown begins to darken his expression but I quickly remedy it.

"Kidding, kidding. Come in."

Relaxing, he runs his gaze over me then back up to my face with a smile. "These are for you." He hands me a stunning bouquet of lilies and daisies.

"Thank you." I inhale their vibrant scent then close the door after he steps in. "Make yourself comfortable. Dinner is about ready, twenty minutes tops. Something to drink?"

"Whatever you've having is fine. What can I help with?" He follows me to the kitchen, resting back against the counter.

"I got it covered, thanks."

Filling a vase with water, I turn back, finally stopping to take him in. His sultry brown hair is styled as though he ran his hands through every piece. The light grey dress shirt does little to hide the stunning male physique of broad, but not too bulky, shoulders and a wide chest. With his hands braced on the counter, his muscular biceps beg to rip through the fabric.

Taking my time, my searing appreciation travels downward to lean hips encased in dark washed jeans, which I already observed grip his firm ass flawlessly.

Yeah—he definitely turns up the heat in the kitchen.

"Do I pass inspection?" he asks in a seductive husk.

My cheeks blush as I drop the bouquet in the vase and turn away, the food suddenly needing my attention. "Yes," I answer softly.

"As do you, every damn time," he speaks in my ear now, pressed against my back, moving the hair off my neck where he nuzzles in. "Smells delicious," he murmurs, running his nose up my neck.

"It's three cheese lasagna," I reply in a lust-fueled whisper.

"I was talking about your skin."

"Oh." The spatula falls from my shaky hands, making a rather loud clang on the counter.

"Turn around." His sinister command has me complying immediately. "So damn beautiful." He traces my jaw with his fingertip, leaning in to place one soft kiss on my lips. "Perfect."

Anticipation looms until one broad, hot hand slinks

down my waist.

"I'm sorry, for everything," I say, needing him to know.

His kiss silences me. It's tender and sweet, his tongue running over my lip seeking entrance, which I instantly grant. He backs me up until I'm flush between him and the wall.

"I need you," I say into his mouth.

His response is a hungry moan, his wandering hands slipping down my thighs past the length of my short dress. My skin tingles under his fingertips as he trails them back up and cups my ass, pulling me even closer, crushing our chests together.

Strong hands grip and lift me up, my legs wrapping around his waist, ankles locking together. My lips glide over his jaw, then gradually up to his ear. "Bedroom," I murmur, needing him, desperate to seal the connection between us.

My hands weave into his hair as he begins to move, turning to turn off the oven—*good thinking*—then carrying me across the room. I dip my head, tilting it to the side, merging our mouths, tongues flicking together with natural passion.

I don't even realize we're near the bed when he bends down, releasing me from his hold as my back meets the mattress. My legs still sealed around his hips, reluctant to let go. He doesn't seem to mind, moving his body with mine until he's standing at the edge of the bed leaning over me.

My hands slide down his back and up underneath his shirt, meeting warm skin, solid muscles flexing under my touch. Slowly he removes my legs, kissing away my pout, and pulls me up to a sitting position.

With a sensual caress over my breasts, tickling slightly along my ribs, he peels the dress over my head. A shiver of pleasure shakes me as I reach for him, deliberately popping each button on his shirt one by one.

Beautiful eyes filled with gentle desire watch me, his head moving forward, dipping down to my bare shoulder, where he presses his mouth. He inhales deeply, his tongue swirling over my skin while I conquer the final button. Opening his shirt, I skim my fingers down rippled abs, smoothing my palms over a strong, chiseled chest, then sliding them back up, appreciating.

Tugging my lips between my teeth, I peer up to eyes glistening with tenderness. He feels it too, wants me as much as I want him. There are no issues, no conflicts, no mess between us. We're in the same arena, but no longer playing any games.

I shuffle back on the bed, leaving him watching me from the end. The air between us is different than any office visits. The intimacy is palpable, and mutual realization of more is understood.

My eyes drink him in as his shirt drops off his broad shoulders and hits the floor. Tugging his belt open, he makes easy work of his pants and steps out, tossing them aside as well until he's only in black boxer briefs, his growing erecting evident, ready for me.

Taking his cue, I reach back and unhook my bra, sliding it down my arms, then raise my hips, hands on my panties, ready to remove them as well when he moves up the bed and catches my wrist, stopping me.

"Let me," he croons.

My smile is relaxed, my heart swelling. He's not just my doctor anymore. He's so much more.

His touch is gentle, feather light, when he parts my

legs and settles between my thighs. Leaning down to press kisses over my hips, then lower, to each side of my panties, he worships me with a hot, seeking mouth before hooking his fingers in the tiny fabric and sliding them down.

"Mhmm." My head falls back, spine arching.

The teasing continues, open mouthed kisses raining down my inner thigh then stopping at my knee, moving to the other leg and skimming back up until his lips graze where the throbbing is nearly audible—my sweltering center aches for him, all of him.

The kiss there is brief, a whisper of a touch, and then he's sliding his body back up over mine. He takes my face in his hands and stares down at me as though I'm a treasure, precious and rare. My leg tangles with his, foot stroking up and down his taut calf, hands raking through his hair and trailing down over his back.

I lift my head and skim my tongue over his bottom lip, where he nips it between his lips, inciting my playful giggle. His erection molds into my thigh and I shift under him, maneuvering so it's right where I need it, upon my center, only a single piece of fabric separating us.

His mouth snares mine, dancing in beautiful rhythm

while my wicked hands move down his side, past his hips, working at his briefs, my feet meeting them half way down and rolling them the rest the way off.

Together, so close, his swollen cock slides against my core.

He rests his forehead against mine, eyes on me, and I know what he needs to hear. What we both want, both feel. It's undeniable and has been for far too long. They're the easiest words I've ever spoken, honest and raw.

"I love you, Brady," I confess in a murmur, tears prickling. My hand seeks his, fingers entwining.

He drags our joined hands up between us and kisses my knuckles with a sigh. "It's always been you, Moe. I've loved you longer than anything else in my life."

With that, he slips inside me, stretching me, filling me, claiming me as his, which I am.

And always have been.

Epilogue
Six Months Later

"SON OF A—"

"Baby," he drops the box he's lugging and rushes to my side, "what happened?"

"I stubbed my damn toe on the table because I couldn't see where I was going. Maybe if I didn't have to take off my damn shoes in your house," I grumble, bending down to rub my foot.

Brady kneels down, taking my foot, massaging the stub, then places a kiss to the top of my toe.

"It's your house too now, love." He stands and moves

behind me, rubbing the sore muscles in my neck. "You can wear mud boots if you want." He bites my ear lobe and whispers low, "And nothing else."

"Mhmm," I purr, letting my head fall back against his chest, toe healed. Something tells me living with Brady will be easy, like *giving* candy to a baby.

"Hello? Where do you want this?"

I quickly unpeel myself from my man as my mother calls out, walking towards us with a large box about to fall from her grip.

"I got it," Brady chuckles, hurrying to relieve her. "Mrs. Porter, please stop. We can get it."

"Brady Reynolds!" She lasers motherly eyes at him. "Just because you're shacking up with my daughter, does not mean you will stop calling me Ellen and I mean it! Mrs. Porter is John's seventy-year-old mother!"

"Yes, ma'am." He lowers his head hiding his amusement.

"Good, now kiss me goodbye, Addison, dear. I have to leave for my doctor's appointment."

"Everything alright?" I asked concerned while taking her in a hug.

"Fine, just routine. Tell your father when they get back with the last load that I've gone. I'm sure he's already forgotten. You kids be good." She pulls Brady in for a quick hug then waves and head out.

We walk behind her, grabbing more boxes when at long last I ask, "Brady?"

"Yeah, babe?" He grunts, lifting a heavy one.

"Are you—" I gulp, deathly afraid of the answer. "My *mother's*…gyno?"

The box slips from his hands as he rears back with a barking laugh, shoulders shaking. "Uh no, not a chance in hell." He grasps my shoulders and moves me out of the way when my brother starts to back another load up to the door. "Watch out!"

Ashley, the way too perfect but very sweet glamour-bot, jumps out of the truck, directing Dylan's attempt at staying off the lawn with the truck.

Brady's chuckle against my temple brings my attention from her back to him.

"Not Ashley's either, babe. "

"I didn't—"

He taps the end of my nose. "I saw that brain

smoking."

He knows me well.

"What about pizza-thieving Blowjob Blondie?"

"Who?" He pulls me fully into his arms

"Candy, *your student* I met that one night."

"Nope, but I gave her my card."

"What?" I slug him in the stomach and start to huff away. "You wait right there, *Dr. Reynolds*. I'm going to get my yearbook!"

"Moe." He snags my elbow and turns me in his arms, pulling me flush against his body. His arms wrap around my waist and slip into my back pockets, giving my ass a tight squeeze. "Look at me."

I refuse, burying a pouting face in his chest, so he kisses the top of my head and continues. "Addison, I have never, nor will I *ever*, cross a line in that office. It was never because it was in that room or taboo or fun for me. It was because it was *you*. Only you, Moe."

My head moves to the side, still resting against his chest.

"I have always loved you and that will never change." His words are strong, honest, leaving no room for doubt.

I lift my head and peer up at him through teary eyes. "Do you love me enough to always take a nurse in the room with you? Not a choice for them, a set rule for you."

"Will that make you happy? Stop you from wondering about every woman we see?"

"It'll help," I pout.

"Then consider it done." He gently cups my cheeks in his hands. "I'd do anything for you, babe. I love you."

"I love you too."

"Oh, before I forget," he reaches into his back pocket with a clever smirk and hands me a business card. "I went ahead and made your next appointment. Date and time are on the back."

Flipping it over, a blush of anticipation ignites. "Very conscientious of you, Dr. Reynolds. I'll see you there."

And in the midst of several pit stops in dark corners, proving time and time again that we can't get enough of each other...somehow, I get moved into our new home.

The End

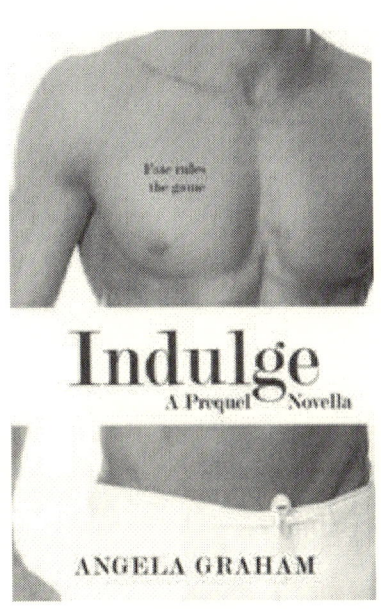

Indulge

Prequel to *The Harmony Series*

Angela Graham

Coming February 10, 2014

Predictable, as always. "Relax, doll." My lip twitched up in a smirk. "I am very much single."

"Oh," she murmured, a pink blush returning to her gaunt cheeks. Her tongue peeked out, skimming her top lip. Her eyes locked on mine as she released the sheet. "In that case…"

My erection grew as I watched her seductive

performance. She ran her fingers down over her breasts as her legs opened, inviting me in.

Unfortunately, I knew better. There was no time. "You can see yourself out."

She wasn't taking no for answer, stepping down from the bed on her tiptoes and strutting toward me confidently. It was one I'd seen far too many times. The morning-after show usually played out one of two ways, but the fact that never changed was that I always had the upper hand. As much as women hated it, I never had a problem turning them away when I was done.

"There's money on the dresser for a taxi."

She released a provoked whine when I turned around and entered my bathroom, closing the door behind me.

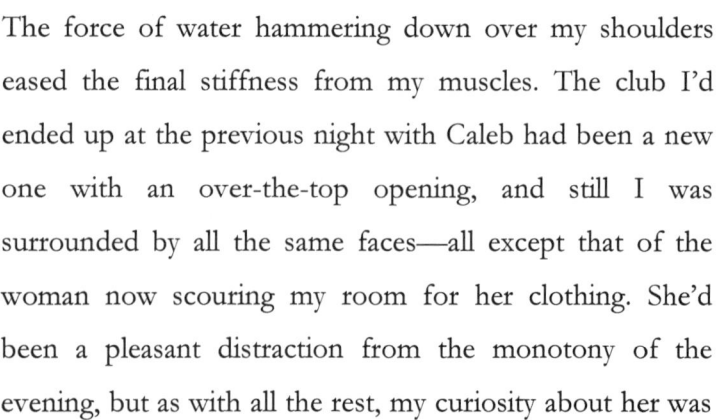

The force of water hammering down over my shoulders eased the final stiffness from my muscles. The club I'd ended up at the previous night with Caleb had been a new one with an over-the-top opening, and still I was surrounded by all the same faces—all except that of the woman now scouring my room for her clothing. She'd been a pleasant distraction from the monotony of the evening, but as with all the rest, my curiosity about her was sated.

The predictable creak of the bathroom door sounded around me as I massaged soap into my scalp. After a quick rinse of my head, I opened my eyes, watching her climb in and shut the shower door.

She gave a sweet-but-far-from-innocent smile, judging by the mischievous gleam in her eye. "I can help," she offered.

She reached for the bar of soap resting on the ledge and lathered it in her hands. I waited, a smirk growing, pleased that like all the others before her, she was eager to make sure I had my fill. Her eyes held mine as she encased my solid erection in her soapy hands and began stroking.

Her tongue peeked out, tracing along her lips as she rinsed the soap away under the spray. A slow smile emerged on her lips and I knew exactly what she was thinking—what she wanted.

"Show me what that pretty mouth can do," I said.

She stooped down on her knees and held my cock firm in her hand. Her tongue swirled around the head a few times, firing my senses to life, before gliding down and swirling around the base. Another lap back up caused my hips to nudge forward, urging her to take me in.

She pulled her gaze from my cock and looked up at me through long, dark lashes before opening her mouth and plunging down over my dick, skimming it over the roof of her mouth. She sucked hard before popping her mouth open and drawing it in again.

Her hand gripped my thigh, digging into the skin while she moved her other hand to the base of my cock, stroking me for added pleasure. I threaded my fingers into her hair, thrusting my hips forward and taking full power.

Her ravishment grew wild, her hand pumping and her mouth taking me deeper, over and over. Her head bobbed frantically. The girl knew what she was doing; she was damn near a pro.

A breath hissed from my lips. "Fuck," I ground out when she scraped her teeth down gently, then slid her tongue back over the sensitive flesh.

I slammed my eyes shut, focusing on the vibrations of her lips humming over my hard cock, nearing release. Her mouth moved faster, rougher. I grasped handfuls of her hair tightly with both hands, holding her lips in place suctioned at the base of my cock as its shaft pumped into the back of her throat.

A rough, gratified moan tore from my throat, clearing

away any lingering stress in my thoughts. My mind was wiped clean as I lost myself in the feeling of her warm lips milking me into my morning release.

The *Evolve* box set by Amazon Best Selling author S.E.Hall includes all four books in the series released thus far: *Emerge, Embrace, Entangled* and *Entice.*

Emerge, Book 1

He lied...my everything I ever knew, trusted, wanted...I am, in fact, without him. On my own and out of my shell, I learn new things about life, friendship and...myself. Like what you've always known may not be what you've always wanted.

Dane Kendrick awakened things within me that I never

knew existed, unraveling and uncovering the real Laney Jo Walker.

I'm a NEW adult...so is my story.

Embrace, **Book 2-**
Evan Allen is a handsome, athletic, southern gentleman who now attends Georgia Southern University for no good reason.

After what he expected to be the romantic gesture of the century, Evan is looking at no friends, a year of ineligibility on the football team, and no girl.

He's starting over alone and doesn't know quite how to proceed. Certain members of The Crew refuse to let him face things by himself, taking him under their wing, and it doesn't take the ladies long to notice him, either.

Sometimes life doesn't go as you had planned. Sometimes it goes better.

Embrace it.

Entangled, Novella 2.5

Things heat up, and not just the Georgia summertime, when Dane and Laney go head to head over plans for her new duplex. But Laney's got his number, and knows just how to coerce her bossy, domineering man. Spend the summer with the gang and find out...just how many is a crowd?

The members of the Evolve Crew are getting older; so is the content. Mature audiences recommended.

Entice, Book 3

Can be read following *Emerge*, *Embrace* and *Entangled* (novella) or as a stand-alone.

Sawyer Beckett does everything full throttle— he's fiercely loyal to his friends, always the life of the party and impossible for the parade of women in and out of his bedroom to forget.

Surrounded by true love and happily ever afters, Sawyer's

not sure if he's enhancing the what-ifs in his head, or if the goddess on stage that night really is worth the search and nagging in his chest.

At the most inopportune moment possible, Emmett Young comes "skipping" back into his life...and for the first time, Sawyer is the one left wanting more. But Emmett can't give her heart; it's already committed—for life.

The only one strong enough to bring the elusive playboy to his knees is the one he can't have. Luckily, Sawyer Beckett doesn't give up easily.

Mature subject matter and strong sexual content- mature audiences only recommended

Connect With S.E. Hall

Twitter: @emergeauthor
Facebook: https://www.facebook.com/S.E.HallAuthorEm
erge
Emerge book trailer, by Lisa at Pixel Pixie:
http://www.youtube.com/watch?v=uWooZtXiQN8
Goodreads: http://bit.ly/19xitqD
Dane facebook:
https://www.facebook.com/DanefromEmerge
Evan facebook: https://www.facebook.com/pages/Evan-
Mitchell-Allen/409174755862025?directed_target_id=0
Sawyer facebook:
https://www.facebook.com/pages/Sawyer-
Beckett/227467650737311
Emerge playlist:
http://www.pinterest.com/emergeauthor/emerge-playlist/
Embrace playlist:
http://www.pinterest.com/emergeauthor/embrace-
playlist/

Other works by S.E. Hall—Emerge on
Amazon http://amzn.to/18nKceN
Amazon UK: http://www.amazon.co.uk/Emerge-Evolve-
Series-ebook/dp/B00CTYIWGO

About Angela Graham

Angela Graham resides in Tipp City, Ohio with her loving husband and three beautiful children. Her first novel, Inevitable, was released in early 2013 and is part of a three book series.

Visit her at Facebook or Amazon!

Made in the USA
Charleston, SC
09 November 2014